soul street

rufus goodwin

soul street

.

FIRST EDITION

Published by Educare Press
PO Box 17222
Seattle, WA 98107

International Standard Book Number: 0944638236.

Library of Congress Cataloging Card Number: 2001087777

Printed in Canada
10 9 8 7 6 5 4 3 2 1

When you consider with your eyes
the visible man, what do you look for?
The man invisible...something is revealed
beneath the gestures, the clothes
he wears.. .and that is the soul.

H.A.Taine
History of English Literature

Don't be croth with uth poor vagabondeth.
People must be amuthed. They can't alwayth
be a learning, nor yet can they alwayth
be a working, they ain't made for it. You
mutht have uth. Do the withe thing and the
kind thing, too, and make the betht of uth;
not the wortht.

Charles Dickens
Hard Times

part one

Crusty, stiff, cold, and sore, bends over the gutter; it is as if God is inspecting the vagrant. They do that in the army: all lined up with their pants off, and the Sergeant barks, "Spread!"

One eye shut, God takes a look. There must be something devilish in it. It is like the scene out of Millet's famous painting, The Reapers, with the harvesters' haunches up in the air against the bare field. But if God is looking at Crusty now, the homeless bum in him isn't aware of it. The Street is not a theology lesson. He is just scrounging for cigarette butts.

In the gutter, lies another crumpled white stump - half-burnt. The stumps of all our days. It is an amazing fact of consumerism that many people toss away their cigarettes after just a puff or two, leaving anywhere from an inch of cigarette behind to a quarter of an inch. If they toss the butts away still lit sometimes the thing burns down inside the paper, of course, leaving just ash. Sometimes not. These empty butts look like cigarettes but are more fool's gold— all appearance, no more smoke. Yesterday's nights. The burned out ends of all our days.

Crusty, veteran tramp, leans over, picks up another butt and slips it into a plastic bag. Already he has a large stash. His back, from all the bending, is hurting. There used to be more tobacco in

9

the stubs, before filters, when a butt still had a real plug in it. Now the stubs are mostly filter, mostly plastic.

People used to suck the weed further down in the old days until they almost burned their lips. They used to enjoy more. Since the filters taste so bad, smokers toss the drag away much sooner. In the old days there was more sweetness in it. People held the butt pinched sideways between their fingernails and balefully drew in the last smoke.

Now it is as if modern folk are frustrated, impatient; they can't get any real smoke, any real nicotine in anyway because of the filters, and they get mad or lose interest after just a couple of puffs and throw the rest of it away before they have any satisfaction. They can't even get real tobacco leaf onto their lips, to spit out, tasting the bitterness. They have forgotten the long drawn out sucking smoke, nursing the weed. It was lighting up that coffin nail that used to count then, in the old days, of course, before all the guilt. Now pleasure is measured by milligrams.

Pulling smokes out of the pocket, in the old days, was as if life itself had a fresh start, at any moment, as if the new kick were an opportunity to start dreaming all over again, fumbling for the matches. Lighting up used to be like having an idea, a sudden inspiration out of the old crushed pack; the packs were paper, not carton; it used to be a cheap way of being one of death's consumers, a 25¢ per pack ticket to a fresh dream as often as you wanted.

Crusty may not remember his own name but he remembers cupping his bare hand against the naked wind, as if making a hut against the elements - lighting the hearth fire. It was almost a mere penny a smoke in the old days. And a man got a light to the end, down to burning his lips. Then the Surgeon General spoiled it all.

In days when smoking was still smart there was some narcotic satisfaction in a real smoke, but then came the plastic filters and the taxes and the tar and the rising price and the Surgeon General's report and the pain.

Crusty was still young in those days; maybe as his former self he still expected to live a decent life; he can't remember that, but the coughing was something awful. Black lung, almost, was what he had. The left bronchial tube was so scorched that it was

10

a bittersweet torture to inhale. The smoke scraped down his throat into his chest like sandpaper roughing over a raw ulcer.

It was a madness. Yet he couldn't get enough of the pain. He couldn't stop. He would wake up in a cold sweat at three o'clock in the morning with the toxic nicotine hangover and think how glad his poor heart was to get a rest– and then, despite himself, go into the bathroom to furtively light up. A midnight puff. Tears came to his eyes knowing what he was doing to himself, before, when life still mattered; yet the misery and pain itself got to be an addiction. He sucked and puffed on his own bitter agony.

That was when he first learned the trade, the butt business. It got so expensive he had to work just to smoke; he began by putting out his own cigarettes after a drag or two, and stuffing the burnt butt back into the pack. It was Lucky Strikes, Pall Malls, and Camels in those days. The strong stuff. Of course, the smoked-out butt was sour the next time around and re-smoking it was like lighting up a mouthful of ashes; then came filters. People started throwing the filter away and Crusty started picking them up, tearing off the filter, and smoking the remainder. At that time he just did it for himself, but it was a turning point. It's hard to say when a man's life turns. Not much always marks the great social divide.

He was, God knows, going to give it up. In fact, he doesn't remember when the first time was, when he first thought of smoking the remains of someone else's cigarette. Second hand drags.

He must have already been toxic. Nicotine poisoning, It probably was outside the old railroad station, where he started hanging out because of the trains coming and going. There were always arrivals and departures and the coffee counter was open late at night. It must have been in the curb outside the station that he first started on second hand smokes. There's always a first time.

Picking up other people's discarded cigarettes is like picking over other people's discarded dreams. Crusty doesn't remember exactly when he graduated, or degraded, but he had stopped buying cigarettes; that was how it happened. He was going to save his lung.

He wishes he could remember now what he was going to save that lung for. What use he had in mind for it. That would be a thing worth knowing. Instead, he started cadging cigarettes. At first it was from people where he washed dishes, but then it was from strangers. "You wouldn't have a spare cigarette, would you?" He remembers that. It wasn't begging. It was cadging. Leaning.

There was a sort of camaraderie in it in the old days. Long ago. Smoking, after all, won the war. Crusty remembers that. It was before drugs. All the soldiers smoked. It was a private's reward. A cigarette was a private's world, the prize of the allies, the compensation of the capitalistic world. It was the way the soldiers made friends. Conquered the enemy. It was society's form of payment. It was the real currency. It was the way the West conquered the world. At Salerno, at Normandy, the GIs arrived floating ashore in cigarette cartons, landing in cigarette packages, and brought down Hitler and Mussolini by lighting up from Sicily to Berlin and blowing clouds of seductive smoke into the eyes of alluring European women in dimly lit cafes across the continent.

Like old movies, it is a long time ago that tobacco was still glamorous, still had its power, and the Indian leaf was still a crop in the Connecticut River Valley. Crusty hadn't yet found that first penny from heaven: a whole crisp, un-smoked cigarette, fresh and white, fallen out of someone's pack on the curb, unlit. That was how it all started, and Crusty looked for more of them, hopefully eyeing the ground, the gutter, but all he saw were butts. Then it dawned on him that he could take the unburnt tobacco from two butts and roll his own.

It was like Edison discovering the electric light. All he had to do was buy the papers and pickup free matches. It was the start of the great skid and it was only another step down to raiding ashtrays.

The only trouble was that the tobacco didn't taste the same. There wasn't the same cachet either, the cellophane, the tinsel, the fresh brand name, the ready made luxury of a pleasure already packaged, purchased, and waiting, The smoke didn't draw as tight and cool through the self-rolled cigarette like it did from a machine cigarette. It didn't taste like a cigarette should. The paper flared up, too, the tobacco leaf was loose, and either it all went up in one quick flame or it burned out. It didn't glow like an ember.

Crusty didn't get that slow, glowing ember, the rising smoke, the dream, from rolled cigarettes the way he did from a fresh pack. The brand name, too, had always done something for him, as if he were puffing on all those advertisements, as if it were a special thing between him and Pall Mall– Pall Mall: no filter, was longer, King size in those days. It was as if Crusty with a brand name had bought into all the advertisement, was part of the cheap picture, part of the hype. That was when he still belonged to the culture, of course.

A cigarette in those days was a brand, while tobacco was still itself just generic. Rolling his own from second hand butts was cheaper, but not as good. The lung got worse. The cough tore him apart. He didn't want to smoke a pipe, so one day he quit cold turkey.

It is the hardest damn thing Crusty has ever done apart from being born, his only other proven achievement in life. He doesn't feel virtuous about it, but it sets him apart, a milestone of withdrawal that he has crossed. He is the veteran of addiction. A former abuser.

Now it is a business. He is an entrepreneur. He has learned it the hard way, off his own habit, but now he is a butt picker and trader. A dealer. Like pickers who deal in old rags, or renderers who reuse fat and cooking oil. He is in the recycling business.

Today he almost has enough in the pouch to take a break and separate the old paper from the raw tobacco, ensconced on a bench, taking his time, the pigeons approaching in their pathetic hope that the filters are something to eat, pecking at them, tossing them around over their beaks.

He bends over, plucks a last butt, and straightens. He looks around to see if there are anymore. Butts are like grubs, these white stubs, like slugs in the concrete and paving of the gutter. His back is stiff. Arthritis and rheumatism are a hazard of the street, of sleeping in the abandoned storefronts, of napping in the gutter, of bending over for butts.

He'll do the ashtrays later, before they empty them. The ashtrays are easy pickings. Quincy Market is not bustling yet. He has the place to himself, with the janitors. The sun is shining. It is dry. That makes a big difference. Rain bleaches the tobacco.

His bench is wrought iron with wooden slats and some of the lamps are still on. Myriads of tiny lights still speckle the bare trees. If only he could remember what he wanted to save that lung for. That would be something.

He can't remember. Crusty, bulky in his clumsy clothes, his puffed parka, settles down in the open breezeway on the bench and sorts through his pouch, He has another one for the raw tobacco. He is organized. He uses his crusty fingernails, thick, yellow and stained, to tear open the cigarette papers and loosen the tobacco with his thumb and flick it into the spare bag. Each butt takes seconds. He throws the filters and paper on the stone walk and soon the pigeons are gathered round, mottled and gray, half of them missing feathers and scroungy, some of them lame.

He has forgotten. He is supposed to put the paper and filters in a trash bag and return them to the dust bin. A bum is not allowed to make a mess.

The pigeons have not been doing too well either during the last two administrations, in the recession; they have no vote, of course, but downtown rot seems to have taken its toll. There are not as many old ladies who feed pigeons as there used to be— with TV, a humane pursuit has gone out of fashion.

Bag ladies are in it for themselves these days and the city has these spikes and electric fences now to keep the pigeons from the ramparts. Tax payer money. Electrocute the birds. Most of them live up under the beams of the green causeway that cuts off the waterfront and only hang around Quincy Market and Faneuil Hall for the fresh crusts of pizza.

Nobody except the bread shops in the North End feeds the birds anymore and half of them are sick and puny. Crusty knows. He and they are in the same business— getting out of the way. Not being trod on. Avoiding the boot. For him and them it is a vocation. A calling.

Crusty, tired from his exertions, like a pigeon, waits for another day and, in search of some scuttling dream, some uplift for the morrow, thinks not of success, fame, or fortune— not even of a woman— but merely of the lost pleasure of smoking, a puff, and a cup of black coffee.

Officer O'Doole saunters brashly up the flagway just as Crusty finishes peeling the paper off the butts. There is a pile of dead filters at his feet and shreds of white cigarette paper. The pigeons scatter as the policeman, beefy in blues, approaches, fingers his gun, and twirls his stick.

"Littering again, are we?" asks Officer O'Doole in a peremptory, academic way, with a slight glint of humor. He makes as if to loose the cuffs at his side, and jangles them.

"Just hustling an honest living," says Crusty, trying to push the filters with his boot under the bench.

"We wouldn't be working, would we?"

"Oh no," Crusty responds. "Not in a public place."

Officer O'Doole holds a white bag in his other hand– coffee and a jelly roll. He looks sheepishly about to see if anyone is looking.

"American enterprise," says Officer O'Doole, motioning to the space beside the homeless man. "I don't suppose as there would be anybody sitting here at this time of day, now would there?"

Crusty looks at the empty space on the bench. Nobody seems to be there. He is quizzical. "No, from the looks of it," he says, and Officer O'Doole sits down heavily. He opens up his white bag and pulls out an extra jelly roll and coffee for Crusty. "You takes it with cream and sugar, I dare say?" Crusty nods. He cracks the plastic coffee lid and feeds the chip, to the pigeons. "Them pigeons got to build their nests," says Crusty, and Officer O'Doole does the same. The grungy pigeons fight for the two wedges and Officer O'Doole looks at them professionally. "There but for the grace of God go I," he says, and Crusty nods, "Amen."

Officer O'Doole asks, "Been saying your prayers?"

"Let the Lord be thanked."

"Attaboy, Crusty. Count your blessings. You live the life of Reilly in the shelter. Sleep in the street. Get free soup. And you're not married to my Rosie."

"Nope," says Crusty, and after a bite of jelly roll he flicks a chunk out to the pigeons.

"Rosie was so mad the other day she walloped me with a pineapple," says O'Doole, looking hurt. "So just to teach her one I handcuffed her and locked her in the closet until she says she's sorry. Do you think I done wrong?"

"Nope," says Crusty, "Rosie deserves it. Take her some flowers."

Officer O'Doole looks gloomy. "When I gives her flowers she thinks I done wrong. 'Been with them prostitutes again?' she says, and won't let go till she finds out what's on my mind."

"Give her chocolates," says Crusty.

"She's already over 300 pounds," groans O'Doole. "How's Crusty?" she asks. "You don't bring Crusty home for supper no more. Me and Crusty, we have a date to go dancing."

Crusty throws the pigeons another smidgin of jelly roll. "Since the recession I don't dance no more," says Crusty.

Officer O'Doole munches on his jelly roll and kicks the pigeons away. "Madeleine?" he says. "How's Madeleine?"

"Inflated uterus," says Crusty. "It's all that air from the subways on the grate where she stands, I say, but she don't listen. She keeps thinking she's pregnant."

Officer O'Doole nods. "I shouldn't ask, but does she still do you in the park?"

Crusty doesn't answer. "You can come down and sleep at the shelter when Rosie acts up," he says. "Be my guest."

"How about a trade. Madeleine for Rosie?"

16

"Madeleine may be a bag lady, but she has her pride," says Crusty. "She used to be a chorus girl."

"I think I seen her down on Washington Street at the old Hoover," says O'Doole, "You know, in the days of the politicos."

"Madeleine was never in the business. She just kicked her legs," says Crusty.

"You should get married," says O'Doole. "Have someone to beg for. Madeleine could pack your lunch. I tell you Crusty, even for a bum, there comes a time to retire. Besides, you'd be pulling two doles instead of one. If you were married housing might even give you a couple of rooms."

Crusty looks glum. "I might have to mow a lawn," he says. "What would I do at home besides watch TV?"

"Well," says O'Doole. "There's me and Rosie. Dinner parties. The Grammys. The Oscars. Public radio. You could come to the annual Policeman's Ball."

He kicks the pigeons again. "These birds is like you, Crusty. They live on the City. Interested in nothing but themselves. They expect old ladies to feed them. A pigeon may spend its life getting out of the way, but in the end it winds up shitting on people."

Crusty looks offended and throws more jelly roll to the birds.

"Rosie still asks about you," says O'Doole. "She says you're the only man in Beantown who still has a soul."

Crusty doesn't answer.

O'Doole kicks the pigeons and says, "Is that true, Crusty. Do you have a soul?"

Crusty looks up at heaven and closes his eyes. That's all O'Doole wants. His soul. That's all they ever want. The soul. That's all a bum has. His soul. It's money in the bank.

"What is the soul, Crusty? If you tell me, I'll tell Rosie. Maybe that will make her happy. Maybe that will save our marriage."

Crusty doesn't answer. He continues to look at the sky with closed eyes.

Officer O'Doole grows impatient. "I'm asking you a question, Crusty, and you're not answering me. I may have to take you in."

Crusty opens his eyes. This has happened before. He has slept in jail in other times. The Irish in O'Doole is unpredictable.

"The soul is a pigeon," says Crusty.

O'Doole flares up, "Don't give me none of that metaphysics," says the officer, unstrapping his gun. He unholsters the .38 and fondles it. "I may shoot myself with this some day," he says, "but first I'm going to get a straight answer from you."

Crusty looks pained. He has been through this before. He throws the last of his jelly roll to the pigeons and squirms uncomfortably.

O'Doole raises the gun. Crusty cringes. O'Doole holds it up, puts it to Crusty's head, and cocks the trigger.

"In the name of the Irish rose, Crusty," says O'Doole, "I want to know in the face of hell whether you have what Rosie says you have or not. Tell me the truth and nothing but the truth, so help me God, Crusty, do you, or don't you, have a soul?"

Crusty, the pistol pointed at his head, looks cross-eyed. He wrings his hands. "Lord help me, I do."

"You're sure, man?" says O'Doole threateningly.

Crusty nods. He raises his right hand as if he were taking oath.

O'Doole begins to haw-haw loudly. "Well, I'll be a skunk's ass," he says lowering the gun. "A man with a soul. In all this great city of ours, one man with a soul. You should be on the force, Crusty. We need a man with a soul. Beantown needs a soul. The world needs a soul. The Church needs a soul. And here you have it and you're out squandering yourself on the street as if God jerked off in a gutter. Hiding your candle in a bushel! It's a shame, man It's a goddamn crying shame."

Crusty looks relieved as Officer O'Doole reholsters his gun. The officer himself looks self-satisfied and reassured, as if all is right with the world. The birds are in their place; God is in his heaven.

He gets up heavily and swats Crusty on the head in a friendly fashion. "You're a lucky bum," says Officer O'Doole. "I'm not taking you in today. Because you have a soul, Godammit. Ha, ha!"

18

Officer O'Doole unwittingly has inspired Crusty with an idea for the day; in the vagrant business an idea is as good as gold. Too many days go by without an idea on the streets of America – real ideas are better than a cup of coffee. The trouble with pigeons is they have no ideas.

So Crusty gets off his duff, routs about, and starts looking for a soapbox. Lots of flimsy orange crates are piled up off the market place, and cardboard cartons, but no real wood. Outside a discount liquor store he finds an old wood wine box that will do, from Spain, and he cautiously tries it out by the ash cans in the alley. He sets it warily down and steps up on the slats. Good as a soap box, too; Crusty gets off it, tucks it under his arm, and heads up to the Capitol.

The trouble with unemployment is there's nothing to do. The money is bad, of course, but it's the languor, the torpor, the lassitude that really eats into a man's soul, the hours of empty boredom, the lack of prospects. Crusty, in his way, is more of an entrepreneur, and now, with his soapbox, O'Doole unsuspecting, has given him an idea.

He heads disconcertedly up past City Hall, that derelict monument that not even money could save, that concrete mausoleum to civic life that not even the best minds in the city could redeem,

19

that cantilevered slab of stone and glass bureaucracy that is a sculpture to spatial lethargy, a mastodon of ineptitude, beside which people, not just Crusty, are reduced to infinitesimal insignificance and inter-personal meaninglessness, the way sardines are reduced by the canning industry.

City Hall is a token of the city monopoly on wealth and ideas. City Hall is the ultimate statement of man's soullessness, the victory of the anonymous metropolis over human flotsam. Not even a souvenir seller or a cup of coffee for sale in the giant, rambling, bricked, alienated square. Not a rag picker or a beggar to boot.

They cleaned it up. Removed the tenements, the life, the riff-raff. No one huddles out here against the rain. No one hawks anything. Bleakness. Desolation. Urban renewal. No more slums. No more people. Just mortar, bricks, concrete, and glass, and inside the monumentality, the bleak piling and processing of government forms.

The city wind funnels here from East, North, South, and West, born to blow people away like pages of a newspaper. All the winds of downtown churn into the plaza in front of City Hall, meet, congregate, and blow everything away. Crusty shivers.

He hobbles on up Beacon Street past the monolithic Bank of Boston high rise, with its many windows overlooking the finance of New England, not to mention the insurance companies, the Prudentials, peering out over Beantown into the actuarial past and future of the region– but nothing in it for Crusty. No homeowner's policy, no liability, no job insurance, no life policy, no death policy, no annuity, nothing but a few quarters in his pocket and all this behemoth of the city to no avail. Just a soapbox, an old wine crate, under his arm.

He passes the First Unitarian Church, dating to the forefathers, still in business, selling salvation, the Beacon on the Hill that brought the message to the New World, but somehow Crusty, along with a lot of others, didn't get it– it never reached him. A pilgrim on the dole? Freedom of worship? No bronze monument to the beggar anyplace, no signpost of salvation to the men like Crusty who inhabit the streets of the New World.

None of this, of course, enters his mind. Crusty's awareness level is dim, very dim. He is not a conscious citizen of our times – a person who votes, who can call the plumber, who buys what he wants, who has achieved individualization in the secular, liberal pluralistic society of modernity, who can buy a car– no he is a beggar. An ancient breed of former cultures, ancient times, other bygone ages, displaced into a modern industrial society, a wasteland, and making a go of it.

He does it. He doesn't think it. Crusty is not aware of being the hero of his own novel, he is not self-conscious.

He is a throwback. An ancient shepherd without sheep. A nomad displaced. Crusty is not the protagonist of a stream-of-consciousness tale that suits the literary pretences of modernism, or escapism, or any other ism. No.

Crusty is an existential fact. A counter. A cipher. The personality reduced to the needs of a physical universe– warmth, shelter, food. A pair of shoes. A hot dog with mustard. A rainless day.

Oblivious of all this, Crusty moves in a primary world, not social references, not structures and opportunities– all that is for someone else. He lives on a sort of vacant moon.

Life is pictures. Writers sometimes get fancy about this kind of thing, speak of Dharma bums, even sentimentalize the tramp– but it is nothing to Crusty. He lives inside the nut. He does not reflect on his condition.

His condition is his existence. He has achieved a sort of integration with survival, a unity of being– but there is no need to sentimentalize it. He has no need of psychologists to sort out the self, the id, the ego. His body and self are one. It is a kind of wisdom that beggars from the beginning of time have had. His face haunts modernity. Mocks the values of our culture. True. But Crusty, no, is not aware of being the hero of his own story.

Instead, he has scavenged the front and back of a banana cardboard carton, made a sandwich sign for himself and crudely painted on the lettering of his homeless slogan, front and back:

I HAVE A SOUL

It is an advertisement for the street self. A protest poster in an impromptu street demonstration that no union, no civic group, no agency organized.

It is a lone placard in the park on the steps of the Commons in front of the Bullfinch capitol dome, with its gold cupola, its neo-classical oratory– and here, in his homemade sandwich placard, not even strutting, standing there like a broken bird, is Crusty: I HAVE A SOUL; I HAVE A SOUL– in front, and behind.

He looks like a protest striker, non-unionized. His is a lone statement. At his feet is a cap laid on the pavement to collect change. Crusty is not doing it for nothing. He is not doing it for the poetry of it.

He is doing it because Officer O'Doole held a pistol to his head this morning and it seems like a good idea. Law and order have funds enough. They have guns. They have cars and lights and sirens. But what does the soul have? Two hands and a pair of feet. A few rags.

No, he is doing it for his lunch. Not for some metaphysical reason, not for some proof of immortality. The soul is a short cup to a bowl of soup.

Crusty stands on his soapbox, plastered with the placard, I HAVE A SOUL, waiting for his hat to fill up with small change. He is not gay, not Lesbian, doesn't have Aids, is not picketing for the union– he is picketing for the soul.

The lone last survivor of the nomad man who still owns his ancient soul. It is Crusty's one personal possession. No tooth brush, no social security card, no TV– just a soul. Invisible. A cause. A ticket to lunch. Advertising the soul is even an employment of sorts, an occupation. A preacher could do worse. He has even heard of Hyde Park, where Crusty imagines all the outcasts of this world making a living on their soapboxes.

He even begins to speak. But no words come forth. No sound. No oratory. He is opening his mouth like a speaker and addressing no less than God, even gesticulating madly, as orators do, poking a finger in the air– but nothing comes forth. It is all gesture and motion. Fury without sound. This speech of the dispossessed. He is in some kind of movie and he has his role to play, mouthing soundlessly: I HAVE A SOUL.

A few hardy by-passers view the spectacle askance, even with a certain amusement, because this absurd speech without words, outside the capitol chambers echoing with their oratory and rhetoric, cuts an absurd, almost comic, yet desperate figure of the soul's place in modern culture– and people pitch a few pennies into Crusty's hat. A penny for the old guy.

It would make a good, old fashioned black and white; a silent movie. The accordion should be playing a tinsel accompaniment.

People, like those scattered onlookers in the park, often think that a man like Crusty will make some long, last terrible noise– not that they want to hear it. Some sound. Like a wail, a cry, a lament.

Something hideous and painful will issue from his throat. It will be like the gnashing of teeth. It will come from within. It will be a prophecy, a Jeremiad. People think this. They think that Crusty will make a sound. A deeply disturbing noise. And then die. Disappear.

But souls like Crusty do not make noise. They are not dogs. They do not bark. They do not bite. They do not make a sound. They are silent. Signs, if anything, of reproach. And they do not die. They do not go away. They hang around. Sometimes they say, "Spare a quarter?" No giant moan issues from them that will change the world.

So he stands there, on his soapbox, with the placard, I HAVE A SOUL, and if it were not for the truth of our times, for the intimidating reality and embarrassment of a derelict in our midst, if it were not for the sad, awful documentariness of this destitute vileness of our society, for the haphazard and brutally cruel demise of a personality, for the mockery of it, Crusty would be a comic spectacle– a sort of stand-up comedian.

This icon of beggar man, a sort of caricature of ourselves, would have a humorous message. A joke to tell. But no one can afford to laugh at the homeless.

Beggars have been, in our most ancient of societies, somehow holy, at least in the East. They wear something of the raiment of God on earth. It is an ill omen to mistreat a beggar, perhaps even a bum. They are part holy, part idiot, part outcast, part scapegoat– walk

23

slow stranger, and avoid the evil eye. It may be the king in disguise, or Siddhartha, or the Bhodissatva, or the Lord himself– certainly not a joke. But Crusty, in the West, no longer has even the dignity of an archetypal outcast; he is merely an inconvenience. A sloppy statistic. A nuisance.

I HAVE A SOUL

At this moment, in the Northern corner of the park, hairy Meathead, the Vietnam veteran from the shelter, with several of his cronies, happens by, on a stroll, looking for action, and happens to spy Crusty on the soapbox with his hat full of coins.

Meathead, his course bulbous nose red in the wind, his windbreaker on, his leather boots scuffed, his horny blue jeans worn and hanging, sees nothing funny about seeing Crusty set up in the park enterprising a few quarters.

"What's this?" he bellows, and the boys shuffle up beside him to have a look at Crusty. Something mean and vicious about Meathead hates that Crusty is working again, bettering his lot; Meathead has a deeply dumb streak in him that rejects and despises enterprise of any kind, indeed, rejects anything but his own brutal, broken down, psychotic, half-dazed animosity to anything unusual or good in life.

Meathead the veteran is the endless bully that cannot accept anything different from himself in life and Crusty, hustling small change with a placard on his back saying I HAVE A SOUL, does not stir any sign of recognition in Meathead, not even envy of the few quarters in Crusty's hat. All Meathead feels is hostility, a kind of senseless rage that Crusty is up to something.

He kicks the hat with the change in it and the boys laugh.

"Working again?" bellows Meathead.

And he gives Crusty a mean shove from off the soapbox, steps beefily up on it himself and crassly announces, "I AM KING OF THE MOUNTAIN!" And he looks belligerently around.

Crusty, like a man with holes in his shoes, picks up his coins. Under the weight of Meathead, the soapbox buckles with a crackle and breaks and nobody dares laugh. Meathead, enraged, begins to stomp on the box, smashing it to bits.

"Goddamn soul," Meathead cries, waving a fist at Crusty. "We'll learn ya who's king of the mountain here . . . ."

24

From the corner of Tremont Street and Park at the Subway stop, two cops on the prowl are walking over to see what the fracas is about. Another day, another dollar.

Crusty hastily peels off his sandwich placard. I HAVE A SOUL. He stuffs it clandestinely in the trash barrel.

Solicitation is not permitted.

Crusty, pigeon-like and habitual in his haunts, in his overused clothes, his usual squalor, is hanging around Park Street Station, a stop on the Boston Commons, this once-grand piece of public planning dedicated in 1639, and faithfully maintained since, though not up to its original standards. Glorious sheep used to graze here. Dashing carriages drove through. Ladies from Beacon Hill traipsed around under their parasols.

The original trees have all been cut, the old picnic spots are gone, the Sunday strollers are no longer in their best. The new Elms have a mournful, seedy, disheveled look, as if they had been planted in the wrong places. There are no grand allees, no stately old oaks. A few neglected baseball fields now, an empty, abandoned boating pond, metal fences, some joggers in plastic stretch suits, but mostly dogs. Girls in baseball hats and sweat suits walk the Beacon Hill canines, the only thoroughbreds left in Boston. The Brahmins are gone.

Occasionally a derelict saxophone player will set up on one of the walkways, on Holidays. Some other people, transients, love couples, slowly traverse the Common's pathways to get from the Capitol to the theater district, or Newbury street, but, unlike in the Garden, there are no flowers, nothing to linger for. No cozy spots. It is as if the founding fathers created the Commons and then

27

forgot about it. It no longer suits the age of the car. Most of the city bypasses.

It is almost as if the Commons in this day and age were in the way, an obstacle to real estate. Overlooked by the capitol, the legislators avoid it. It is a public space that has forgotten its mission.

Up at the head of Park Street is the regal seat of government, the steps, the Gold Dome. It looks embarrassed to be there, as if someone transported a building from Europe and misplaced it. Formally, it is an imitation of grandeur. The rhetoric is there, the columns, the black wrought iron fences, the steps, but not the audience. The monumentality is a presence, not the people. It is as if the bright leaf had turned into fool's gold, a replica of the past, which nobody believes is real any longer.

Not even Crusty, still inclined to believe in some things, living, as he does, in this national citadel of culture and moral purpose. The City on the Hill.

The center of action, instead, is the donut shop. The whole Eastern side of the commons along Tremont Street is a movie set of an inner city. Minorities hang here, and there is a boarded up Vietnamese restaurant, a dilapidated town tower that is now a fast tenant turnover, a dollar bargain store, discount shops, souvenir, postcard and trinket stores. A few street vendors. A policeman. A bus stop. Pretzels. The Subway. And the ubiquitous Crusty.

He sometimes catches the crowd coming in to shop on Washington Street at Filenes and Jordan Marsh's, but today the policeman is a young one who doesn't know him, and Crusty ambles away from him up Park Street.

Beyond the Paulist Fathers, who now have a corner on the Commons and hawk books of salvation, there is a sign out: "LUNCHEON TODAY."

It is outside a large, once elegant town house, with a recessed stoop leading up to an arched door; it is the Union Club; it has a privileged, complacent feel about it, and Crusty is hungry. He wonders what is on the menu.

It is early already but a few properly suited guests are arriving one by one at the club, raincoats alike, some young professional

28

graduates, others obscure pillars of society, men of affairs, sorts that Crusty doesn't often see, and he wonders if his bag lady, Madeleine, is out in the park.

She often feeds the pigeons at lunchtime. It is her hobby. She picks up the old bread on Charles Street, in her bandana, her motley woolen bathrobe, her baggy leggings, her old slippers, warts on her face, her cart and assortment of old bottles, cans, and trash, and she eats from the same crusts as the pigeons. She always offers Crusty a part and sometimes even has stale cheese. If she is flush she brings beer and baloney.

Crusty, by the Union Club, doesn't at first see Lowry, ample though he is, in his short brimmed canvas hat, his brown suit, raincoat and black shoes, Lowry is puffing from the walk, out of condition, slightly larger than life, stops a moment, and looks across the street.

There stands Crusty, propped up against the iron rail, next to the Luncheon Today sign.

It is not the first time Lowry has seen this bum. He seems to have seen him several times, at Copley Square, in the theater district, maybe on Charles Street. He recognizes the face, the stubble, the square jaw, like a Rembrandt portrait— that's what he noticed. Crusty has a shirking shoulder, too, like a man who expects a blow and has been hit once too often. Why else does Lowry remember him?

Perhaps because Crusty looks like Lowry's grandfather. He looks diabetic, red-nosed, raw skinned, broken vesicles on his face, sawed off hair, bony, crusted over, although Lowry's grandfather wasn't shabby. Lowry rests for a moment, gazing at Crusty, studying him, remembering his own grandfather who used to give the crippled vagrants on the street his small change when he took Lowry for walks with his cane. A man could do better in those days. The standard handout was a dime, and that got coffee. Today the rap is a quarter, but coffee costs seventy-five cents.

Lowry, looking at Crusty, thinks how well his own hedge fund is doing. His grandfather would be surprised. So would this bum. Money is amazing. He is talking not millions of dollars, but hundreds of millions. Actually, the European and Japanese bonds this year could turn it into a billion dollar year. The minimum wage may be 4.40 an hour but another world is afloat in greenbacks.

Lowry correctly bet that foreign interest rates would fall, as domestic rates had, driving up the value. He was there in global bonds at the right time with everything he could get a hold of.

He wasn't quite up there with Mr. Soros, Steinhardt, Robinson, or Omega, the legendary stock pickers, and he didn't get in on Paramount, but he was ahead on Medco before Merck moved in, and he followed Omega into soybeans. But it is the global bond business that put his hedge, Brahmin Investors, into the billion dollar range. Pure profits. High risk.

This, while out there the rest of the world is coming off the recession. His grandfather wouldn't have approved. Yet he himself is still optimistic. That's why Crusty, like an omen, bothers him.

A hedge fund can only have ninety-nine investors, so it goes without saying they have to have substantial assets and be able to absorb the risk. Crusty reminds him of the risk. Each investor has to pony up the quota, at least a million, but some are much larger, and Lowry borrowed heavily to make a killing. He has his own money in, the institutional investors pay a one percent management fee and everybody pays twenty per cent of the profits.

Risk. That's why he is looking at Crusty, as if at a portrait in the Fine Arts Museum. Lowry's grandfather would have handed Crusty some spare change and called it a day, still proud of his Sunday best, sure of his house on Beacon Hill. Lowry, instead, examining Crusty from afar, even thinks he has dreamed of this man. The cut of Crusty's jaw is unforgettable.

Like the financial market, Lowry thinks, the earth is a constant motion that somehow holds itself up, and, because the earth does it, he too, Lowry, has to be somehow constantly holding the thing up, constantly straining. This is why Rockefeller put the statue of Atlas shouldering the world in at Rockefeller center, but Crusty there, across the street, has let go— he doesn't hold the world up, yet the world still hangs there in space, still spins, and there is Crusty too. People do so much. Just to live. But there is Crusty, alive despite it all, defying survival.

"By God!" Lowry says to himself.

He strides across the street, right up to the homeless man.

"What's your name, man?"

"Crusty."

"You're coming to lunch," Lowry says gruffly, taking him by the elbow. "Be my guest."

Crusty thinks with alarm of his bag lady; she'll be waiting with the baloney. He shrugs and paws with his boot. The stained jacket crinkles on him. This big man, this Brahmin, is about his same age. Lunch? Who is he kidding? But Lowry has him by the elbow. "It's on me," he growls. "Never mind. Just stick with me. I'll handle them. It's not everyday a Roosevelt speaks."

Crusty is reluctant, but Lowry is big, importunate. "It's a handout," Lowry tells him, gruffly coddling him along. "Just look like a Brahmin."

Lowry shuffles him up the steps, number eight Park Street, and together they enter the distinguished building which, like both of them, has seen better days. Something of the nineteenth century still possesses this town, a patina of the historic, and there is no doubt all these men, young and old, are college grads. All but a few are in fine suits, yet with something of the classroom still about them. They have never quite outgrown the ivy walls.

Yet it isn't so tweedy, clubby, and comfortable as it once was. The blue jeans, leather jackets, and baseball hats of Park Street Station are the real world now. The times have outstripped the old Brahmins and everything, including the rich, are more ragged.

Besides, these luncheons for gubernatorial candidates mostly draw people from the closet who in the recesses of their secret minds think they themselves should be governor. It comes somehow with the turf, higher education. They have civic dreams of grandeur and identify with the chief.

Mostly this crowd is Beacon Hill, Cambridge, Commonwealth Avenue. The hall is not grand, but opens into a fireplace sitting room on the right, a reading room on the left. Straight ahead is the billiards room.

Wursell, the Middlebury man, a former jock, is at the desk taking names and Lowry shoves forward.

"College?" Wursell asks.

"Amherst."

Wursell writes, and then looks up. It is Lowry, of course. He knows him.

"Make it two," mutters Lowry, while the hapless Crusty stands meekly beside him.

Wursell raises his eyebrows.

"Two, I said," Lowry repeats, and Wursell swallows. Lowry is a bona fide Brahmin, President of the Urban Defense League, a governor of City Hospital, and a descendant of John Winthrop of the Mayflower days. He has a bow tie on and a scowl.

Wursell, annoyed, is looking at Crusty and waiting. His pen is poised on the list. "College?" he repeats.

Lowry looks at Crusty and guffaws. Crusty looks at the floor.

Lowry turns to Wursell. "Dr. Crusty is doing research for MIT. Here's an extra eighteen dollars for him."

Lowry almost laughs again. An L.D., Doctor of Life. The streets. Pine Street Inn. A diploma of down and out. The baccalaureate of the gutter.

Wursell feels an absurd need to say something. There were times when a man had to have a tie, he thinks, but Lowry moves on the drinks. The table is set up with gleaming glasses bottoms up, and the gray haired butler– what used to be called a retainer– is hobbling around behind the table which offers fruit juice, tomato juice, and wine.

To Crusty, who looks like someone just out of a manhole, Lowry says, "Have some wine. On the house."

Guests back away as Lowry pushes Crusty up to the hors d'oeuvres, all except Dorothy Lamson, in her chemise suit, and Lowry says, "Dorothy, this is Dr. Crusty. He's coming to lunch."

"Be our guest," Dorothy says, "It's long overdue."

Crusty grunts. "What college do you come from?" he says, parroting Wursell.

"Smith," she laughs. Crusty smells. These must be the same clothes he has had on for a year. Dorothy tries to think of something funny to say, but fails. "How is the food they give you?" she asks.

"Street gourmet," Crusty says.

"They feed him like a king," Lowry tells her, slamming Crusty on the shoulders. "Better than the lunch we're going to get."

"They usually have baloney. It's a political lunch," says Dorothy.

Crusty thinks forlornly of Madeleine. She'll feed his portion to the pigeons. The birds like some fat.

"Where's that photographer?" asks Lowry. "This is a picture I'd like to have."

He looks around at the walls. Nineteenth century lithographs—Edward Everett, former governor, Brigadier Howells, a pugnacious civil war commander. There are chandeliers and red carpets. Lowry wishes he could find that Peace Corps veteran. He would talk to Crusty.

They move upstairs early to get a table up front in the 2nd floor dining room overlooking the park. More lithographs. Dark moulding. White table clothes. The service is buffet, and sure enough it is baloney. There's also some roast beef, pressed turkey slices, a cabbage soup, and salad. At least Dorothy sticks to Lowry; with Lowry's girth, and Crusty's jacket, they seem to take up six places at the table. Four other people are already seated, and their eyes bulge when they see Lowry seating Crusty.

"James Lowry," Lowry says to them, "Brahmin Investors, Dorothy Lamson. And this is Dr. Crusty. He came especially to hear what Mark Roosevelt has to say."

Two couples cringe and look like, well, you how who has come to dinner. Crusty plunks down with his plate and starts to eat his baloney. There are waitresses offering coffee. Nobody talks about the weather.

Lowry tries a joke. "Did you ever hear this one? A bum walks up to a man on the street and says, 'Could you spare a hundred and forty dollars for a cup of coffee?' The man says, 'Coffee's a quarter.' The bum says, 'I know, but I couldn't go into a restaurant dressed like this.'"

Nobody laughs. Nobody even smiles, except for Crusty, who grins, his broken front teeth showing.

Lowry tries again. "Two bums," he says, "were brought to court for vagrancy. The judge asked the first, 'Don't you have a home?'

The bum says, 'I live in the countryside. Sometimes I just bunk down on the beach.' The judge turns to the second bum. 'Where do you live?' The second bum answers, 'Next door to him.' "

Crusty grins again. Everybody else stares dumbly at Lowry. "What is this?" Lowry asks, "a funeral? Don't alumni know anything besides rah-rah and investments?"

"Maybe Crusty knows a joke," Dorothy suggests.

All Crusty can remember is the one about the man standing outside a restaurant with a cap in each hand, if he can remember it correctly. Someone asks, "Why do you have two caps?" The bum answers, "Business is so good, I've opened a branch office."

But he doesn't tell this one. He repeats one he heard from Meathead, in the shelter. "What's the difference between a porcupine and a Cadillac?" he asks Lowry.

"I don't know."

"With a Cadillac the pricks are on the inside," says Crusty.

He should have told the other one, but Lowry, who has a Cadillac himself, guffaws and Dorothy smiles on her baloney. The waitress serves Crusty his coffee.

Bert, an ivy-league black, assistant chief of staff to Mark Roosevelt, is about to introduce the candidate for governor. Bert is the only black in the room, no Hispanics either. Roosevelt, 38, represents Beacon Hill and Backbay in the state legislature, but his chances for governor are slim.

This great grandson of Teddy Roosevelt, and grand nephew of FDR, gets up in his blue shirtsleeves. He says the last time he overtalked because he didn't have his watch– only a calendar on the wall, ha ha, and then he asks a question: "Who in this room today believes that our children will actually have a better life and more opportunity than we have had?"

There is an uncomfortable silence. Some shuffling. Then Crusty raises his hand. He is the only person out of sixty or more listeners to do so.

But he keeps his arm aloft.

Roosevelt, who wrote the Massachusetts education reform bill, says the state is fiftieth in the union in per capita spending for education, on a par with Thailand. In places like formerly industrial

Lowell, he points out, the biggest slice of the action is in the illegal economy, and now leadership wants to balance the budget by putting in casinos.

Casinos expect those who are on welfare and in illegal economies to lose 1,200 dollars each a year to sustain the state. Instead, Roosevelt favors total overhaul of the social welfare to support those who help themselves– by low paying jobs, living with the family, or marrying– but would use the "family photo" to refuse supporting further children.

The deterioration of America, alarmingly, is not just an economic thing, he says, and he speaks movingly of upgrading the public dialogue and pleads for the telling of truth as an antidote to the politicos always saying only what they already know people want to hear. Naturally, he will lose the election.

There are questions and finally Lowry elbows Crusty. "It's your turn," Lowry says and raises his hand for Crusty. Roosevelt points in their direction.

"Crusty has a question," Lowry announces, prodding the homeless man.

Everybody waits.

What is the question fifty years after the Great Depression and the era of FDR at a Union Club luncheon honoring a man who calls himself Roosevelt? It is like Parsifal at the castle of the Grail: the question– if he does not ask the right question, the Fisher King will not be cured of his mysterious wound. The kingdom will not be healed. The Alumni are waiting.

Crusty looks at Lowry. There is nothing such as a free lunch. Wherever you go, there is a price to pay. That is the system. Baloney isn't free.

"Come on," says Lowry, "the governor is waiting."

The Alumni lean forward. They are afraid of the question, that it will be about them. They are afraid that the voice of the social depths will reveal the abyss of social dislocation, will be a threat, an accusation. Lowry wonders if Crusty's chapped mouth will expose as a sham and ridicule the fragile, brittle superstructure of suburban lives, their offices, their polished shoes. Will some whimper, some moan, some roar convulse the luncheon?

Crusty coughs.

He clears his throat. Then he asks Mark Roosevelt up at the podium something that everybody else in the room has been thinking since they sat down.

"Maybe you could tell, your honor," says Crusty, straining hoarsely under the unaccustomed burden of public speaking, "Why the lunch wasn't hot?"

The oracle has spoken. Beef Stroganoff. There should have been Beef Stroganoff. With all the talk of education reform, of SAT scores, of disparate township spending, of upgrading the dialogue, Crusty has asked the honest question that everybody else in their pin-striped breeding had thought looking into their own plates of baloney and cold cuts.

In the room there is a titter, a ripple of relief, some light laughter. Lowry gazes at Crusty proudly. As they applaud, young Mark Roosevelt, great grandson of Teddy, grand nephew of FDR, looks around the room thinking of his ancestors.

Someone pushes up to the podium and asks for his autograph on the program. "In the hope that all goes well," he writes.

No one asks for Crusty's autograph. Lowry puts an arm around him to protect him and Dorothy Lamson shakes his hand. "It's an honor to meet an American," she says to him.

"It's a pleasure to oblige, Ma'am," says Crusty, before heading out.

Lowry feels foolish at the curb, but Crusty is back home. The would-be billionaire looks at the luncheon bum and knows he has forgotten something. The homeless man has a secret. That is it. A story.

Not the Sermon on the Mount, something simpler. Where has he come from? How has he crossed over? Perhaps it is that.

But maybe it is something even more crucial. Lowry knows nothing of Crusty's secret love. Lowry has no secret love. Whatever it is, Lowry is missing out on it. In fact, he doesn't even know what to say. That bothers him.

Neither does he want to steal the man's story. It doesn't sound like Crusty has much else that is his own. Maybe that is his secret. How much, in fact, is the story of a man's life worth?

36

Lowry pulls a 20 dollar bill out of his wallet and gives it to Crusty. Crusty begins to refuse, but Lowry pushes it on him. A miserable twenty. But the money is like a cheap option on the bum's tale, and Lowry isn't sure he has enough money or anything else to really pay for that.

He hails a cab.

"Drop you off?" Lowry asks, half in fun.

"No," says Crusty, "I'm home."

Lowry thinks of the sign down on the Starrow drive apartments, "If you lived here, you'd already be home."

Crusty, on the curb, has already arrived. Poverty is a short trip. Or is it a long detour?

Crusty holds the cab door for him. He has seen it in the movies. Lowry is thinking of his grandfather. Luxury is being able to remember your own ancestors.

The cab moves up Park Street, the high back of the partition obscuring the driver so that Lowry is a crammed prisoner in the back separated from the world by Plexiglas.

"I just had lunch with Mark Roosevelt," Lowry says.

"Who's that?" asks the cabbie. Lowry can't see if he is foreign.

"Candidate for governor. Young guy. Very articulate."

"Oh yeah," says the cabbie. "They have to be articulate. First lie, then take the money, then vanish."

Must be an American. Pakistanis don't understand our politics. The meter ticks. But Lowry is watching the capitol go by and no longer thinking of his grandfather, but of Crusty.

An omen. It galls him.

Lowry sits at his mahogany desk down the hall, at the corner, facing the window.

It is the 27th floor of the International Trade Towers, the twin Romanesque modern tinsel toy scrapers West of Fort Point Channel. They never did build the new urban center out on Dock Four, so the view of the harbor is unimpeded.

The only thing the view lacks is a bridge over to East Boston, but the span is too great. They're building the third tunnel instead. It will take them until after the year two thousand, probably be late, and cost even more than Lowry himself has at risk in bonds.

His desk has nothing on it. He can enjoy the view, but the Tall Ships are gone. He misses them. His business seems to have peaked about that time, but now he has debts. Perhaps it is time to retire. Cut the losses, bail out at the top, retreat to Beacon Hill and enjoy the money.

It would be better than looking at Boston Harbor, admirable as it can be, gnawed by a urge to jump out the window. Fortunately, they are sealed. It is always best to contain this urge and go to the bathroom instead. Perhaps he should put a photo on the table— money isn't the only thing. His son– the generation X-er. Lunch is even better than jumping out the window. He knows that. Still the millions pile up.

Now even Crusty owes him a lunch.

Lowry can't figure out why he took the man to the Union Club. Certainly it couldn't have been pleasant for Crusty, nor was it entirely pleasant for Lowry– he began to have the feeling he was not entirely safe.

The Alumni were mostly younger than he was, Crusty himself a cipher. Then there was his inexplicable impulse to take Crusty in, to slam him on the back, to josh him. He had been avuncular and patronizing. He had counted on his Brahmin credentials to get them through the line.

His putting Crusty on at the Club had really been some expression of his attitude towards the Alumni, almost a prank, some kind of disdain of the very customs that he counted on to keep himself afloat, fully invested, in a hedge fund, up on Beacon Hill.

Yet he wouldn't think of saying to Crusty, "Go jump out of the window." He wouldn't even say it to the Alumni. What if somebody actually did a thing like that? He shuddered. That was why he was in it for the money.

He knows he has seen the man elsewhere in the city, under an archway, a passage, more than once, in fact, and remembers approaching but imagining that he jumped him, maybe strangled him. He thinks he did it for some kind of pleasure, rather than for the money– which seems to him strange, because spare change is important to Lowry.

The value is why he is wary; he is no longer sure himself whether a quarter or a million is worth more. Besides, the truth is, he thinks somebody else should take care of these people. But Crusty puzzles him.

It is not everyone he invites to lunch. The strange thing is that since taking Crusty to lunch, he has begun to think of killing him. This is not like Lowry. He sometimes thinks of eliminating the homeless, but not killing them. There is no one to talk to about this. He lives with his son. He would never admit a thing like this to his son.

His son is entering generation X. He knows everything already, and like the rest of them, is trying to be different. Lowry doesn't admire him. He pities him. He knows that no matter how hard his son tries, they won't let him be much different from the rest. On the other hand, he doesn't want him to end up like Crusty either.

Still, Crusty can walk. Lowry's grandfather died in a wheelchair. Perhaps, Lowry thinks, he was lucky. He went bankrupt, crippled, and recluse thus keeping his fortune, his wife, and his house and passing it on. Hopefully, this gave him some pleasure. Otherwise he might have ended like Crusty.

In fact, was this why Lowry himself, haunted by his grandfather giving the bums spare change, had gotten into the hedge fund in the first place? He remembers the streets, with his creased shorts, jacket, and necktie, his polished shoes, his big eyes, his new haircut, soaped, pink, hands washed, walking back to the town house and seeing the littered bodies of alcoholic beggary slumped on the stoops, draped on the curb, and first being aware of himself.

"There go I." It was his first tangible picture of the future. He wondered how it could be that he would go from granddad's town house to the gutter.

How could his life, barely begun, find such a seemingly long route from wealth to penury, though he saw it at the time as a trip from short pants and parted hair to rags and grubbiness. From the parlor to filth. From warmth and childhood to this terrible sadness that threatened to be– himself.

Now, of course, Lowry knows that Crusty's fate is only two or three paychecks away, maybe ten, maybe fifty. In his own case it could be overnight. He is not exactly what you call a working man. He knows that. Yet still Crusty puzzles him. Still, he wants to kill him.

The thing about Crusty is his jacket. It's a baggy, synthetic fiber, lined, water-repellent , blue-gray, all-purpose job with multi-pockets inside and out, a drawstring, and three-quarter length. It must be warm. Good for sleeping. A cushion even.

Lowry wonders where he gets a jacket like that, if he's a bum, although Lowry himself has one like that. He got it at Larkin's, the gentlemen's clothiers.

Crusty's boots are patent leather work shoes, with soles and heels, light brown, with laces. Only his pants look really soiled. But even they are double-duty cotton, workplace fabric, torn maybe but quality.

Lowry should ask his grandfather. Or his grandmother. Maybe she would know. After all, she told him how to stop a bloody nose with a twist of toilet paper, although she wouldn't do it herself. A chorus girl. Blond. Oval face. Makeup, doted on granddad.

Of course, by that time granddad was crumpled down, six inches shorter, head still erect, neck bullish, ruddy, master of a wheelchair. She brought him his cards. His books. His desk was the tray that swung over his blanketed knees, all tucked in, the legs gone, and he was allowed to play solitaire.

She had a voice of cream, but never showed her legs anymore. Her dresses were a cross between the matron, the actress, and the nurse– no way, anymore, of telling if they were elegant, dowdy, or plain efficient. Yet he didn't seem cowed by her. He still had the temper. Nor did she seem ashamed of him. Wherever she came from. She even wheeled him to the theater, which is what he was still supposed to like, because the actors and actresses still had legs. Vicarious walking.

All that money. Granddad saved a fortune by going bankrupt, ignominious as it was, or else he would have gone the way of Crusty, at least without her. He lost his horses, his office, and everything that she liked to be, but she encased him in dignity all the same, even though he had to face everyone left in his life without his legs, and knowing he was bust. He didn't flinch from it. But she kept him cozy.

She wasn't at the hospital the last time Lowry saw him. She wasn't even at the funeral, as far as he could remember. The room was bare, white, the bed high, imposing, and he couldn't scarcely see the square head, the salt-and-pepper hair, the stocky expression of dauntingness. The linen spread was smooth. All was quiet. The tubes trailed into his nostrils; the intravenous dripped into his arm. It all seemed fragile, infinitely delicate. Macabre. Far from the stage door. Far from the polo field. Far from the bank. Maybe she was at the lawyer's.

She wasn't even his first wife. She had no issue in it. Afterwards, she would almost disappear. Her only real contact after that was with the bastard, the gay one, who showed up at the funeral in a Hawaiian shirt only to hear the will read.

But Lowry's real current nightmare is not granddad, not Crusty, but the security system.

He spends half his working days wondering how to get into his own office.

He has the key, of course. He has cards. He has a password. He has a number. If he forgets anyone of these, he is locked out.

He has to sign in; he has to sign out.

The system is perfect. There is no loophole. Even his car is safe. He has thought it through a million times. Traced every step to his door from every possible entrance and found no way to get past the locks, the guards, the alarms, and the automatic doors.

For instance, he approaches. Not smiling, acceptably dressed, nearing the security desk with a certain aplomb, wary, getting his greeting ready, careful not to be overly jaunty, trying not to look too put out, not depressed gauging his speed, trying to remember his social security number, his license ID, his bank account serial, his digits, his license plate, his Pin number, the name of his insurance agent, the address and his telephone numbers, the name of his doctor, and other urgent information, and the deskman challenges him.

"Hi!" the deskman says, between the fire alarm, the phone, the garage monitor, the sign-in book, the parcel drawer, the house register, the alarm system, and the newspaper.

Lowry hesitates.

"How are you?" the deskman adds.

He hasn't been quick enough, Lowry hasn't. He was debating between answering, "Hi," or "Hullo."

He grunts. He is supposed to say, "Very well, thank you." his banker has clued him in on that, but again he hesitates: "Fine?" "Okay?" "Good" or, "Not good?"

Again, he is not quick enough. It is amazing to think that he is in for a billion dollars but that he still isn't quick enough to get by the guard. He is about to open his mouth, but the guard says, "Which unit are you, Sir?"

Suddenly he cannot remember his own office door. The numbers are there, but they seem to be blurred. He sees his own door plainly enough, on the 27th floor, and this might save him. "27th floor," he could have said.

Instead, he says, "Lowry."

"Lowry is not in," the deskman answers.

A hidden fear seizes him. He should have said, "I am Lowry," but the deskman is too quick for him again and says, "Lowry is out."

Now his line is, "You don't understand. Mr. Lowry is myself." But this seems beneath him. It is a clumsy line. Not dignified. He hesitates again.

"Who shall I say is calling?" asks the guard.

This is so patently absurd that Lowry becomes annoyed and thinks how much older he is than the guard, but he also feels guilty, because the guard is working for his money, and his grandfather told him to never question the value of a man's labor, but not to be recognized is also insulting, and he thinks, "The Devil!"

The guard looks alarmed. He presses a buzzer.

Another guard shows up.

Lowry says to him, "Hi," meekly, almost, but it is too late. "What's wrong?" asks the third guard.

"This man says he wants to see Lowry," says the deskman. This is not true. He never said that. He is Lowry. But he failed to say that. Another mistake, and he will be out on the street.

"What do you want?" says the new guard.

This, suddenly, is the absurdest question Lowry has ever heard. He wants to be Lowry. Or does he? All his life he has wanted something, but no one has ever asked him what he wanted. Either they gave it to him or he took it. But there never was much question about wanting or not wanting. Now the only answer he can think of is, "To be Lowry," but if he says that the guards will either think he isn't Lowry or that he is crazy.

"Why doesn't he answer?" the first guard says to the second guard.

"I don't know," the other man says. Then he says to Lowry, "Have you got your passcard?"

Lowry whips out the passcard and hands it to the guard.

"Thank you," says the guard, looks at it, and passes it to the first guard. The first guard takes it, checks it, and puts it down.

"What about your license?" says the second guard.

Automatically, Lowry reaches for his license. It is like a reflex. But then he thinks. They already have his passcard. Now they want his license too. He holds onto it.

The guard waits impatiently. Other than his credit cards, this is the only proof that Lowry has on him that he is himself. The rest is at home. He looks at the guard half-pleadingly, half-trusting, but the man is implacable. He is holding his hand out. With a sinking heart, Lowry passes him the license, the guard hands it without looking to the deskman, who looks it over.

"Lowry," the deskman reads. "James. This belongs to Lowry." He looks up quizzically at the second guard.

Lowry is almost angry. "Lowry," he says, "James Lowry. It says so right on it."

The second guard glances at the deskman. "He says it belongs to Lowry," he says.

Now Lowry's mind is racing. He should have said, "Mine. It's mine, mine, mine!" But he has been taught not to be possessive. Me was a dirty word in his upbringing.

"Are you Lowry?" the second guard now asks him.

What an insult. Of course he is Lowry. "Of course," he says.

The first guard says quietly, "He claims to be Lowry."

Now Lowry glowers at both guards. The guards eye him and look at each other. It seems to be an impasse, but then Lowry begins to wonder if he is really himself. Immediately the guards look suspicious. This building. This money. This security system. Maybe it's all Crusty's fault. Maybe he's just another Crusty.

Taking the elevator up to the 27th floor, walking down the carpeted corridor to the door whose number he has suddenly forgotten, is this what his grandfather wanted for him when he gave spare change to those bums lying in the gutter, and Lowry, looking at them, saw himself?

Is the true Lowry, the man in it now for a billion, the man still living on Beacon Hill, the father of a generation X-er, the governor of the hospital, the member of the boards, the luncheon guest at the Union Club, really an imposter?

Is he the man really on the license, the man on the credit cards, the man now overlooking Boston Harbor?

Perhaps. Some of the water is almost blue. Somebody is sailing. Clouds are scudding in the sky. Perhaps he is himself. But the guards might not think so; they might continue.

First guard: "Maybe he's not Lowry. Does anybody in the building know him?"

Second guard, to Lowry: "Do you know anybody in this building?"

Lowry hesitates. He doesn't want to bother anyone. Besides, it's preposterous. He still hesitates. The fact is Lowry has not associated much with anyone in the building. He has been too busy making money. He knows who the president of the Towers is, but also knows the man is sometimes unreliable. A practical joker. He just might, for the fun of it, deny knowing Lowry. There are others that Lowry has slighted in some obscure way or another— what if one of them was jealous of his billion, and out of spite, said, no, he was not Lowry? He was Crusty!

Worst of all, what if he wasn't looking like himself. That very morning he had scarcely recognized the balding, fattening, wrinkled, paunchy man he had become in his own mirror. Why should anyone else recognize him? This was not a cheerful thought. He was about to mention the name of one of the partners in a suite down the hall from his own offices, when the guard says, "Do you have any scars to prove who you are? Appendix? Gall bladder? Anything?"

Lowry has no scars. He has lived a charmed life. He has never bashed his head open. Never gone through the windshield. Never fallen downstairs. Never been in a knife fight. Never been burned. All he has to show for his days on earth is money. Even his son wonders who he is. That, and his dignity. But the guards make about 12.50 an hour and, instead of dignity, they wear uniforms. Why should they care?

"Maybe we should call a doctor," says the first guard.

"Or the police," says the other.

Lowry looks out the window. He has three alternatives, he realizes– wait for the doctor, get out of the building, and, or, call the police himself.

He smiles. This has not occurred to him before. In fact, Lowry never has called the police, not even when his own wife threatened him with an axe. Not even when he was robbed. Not when they broke into his house. Not when they busted into his car. He never even called the police when they ran into his car– the police came by themselves.

He ponders on this. He associates the police with open manholes and traffic jams. Presidential parades, maybe. Jails. Crime. Not with anyone he knows, anyone he loves. Not with himself.

Not even with Crusty.

In that slow, dim-witted way of his, Crusty, not because he is natively dumb, but because his mind is bogged down by the sheerness of survival, notices that Spring is coming. He wraps up and is out on the Commons. Most people notice Spring because they expect it; March twenty first approaches and they see it coming on a calendar. Crusty does not function by calendar.

Spring is no longer for him a season of schedule. His life is demoted to dull, primary sensations. Because his threshold of perception is reduced, it takes a lot longer for him to notice and be aware even of ordinary things. But he is out in the Commons this day, sitting placidly on a bench, and it suddenly has gotten warmer.

By chance he sees a poster. It says, "The World of Color," and shows a giant close-up of irises.

It is a bright picture and Crusty studies it for a long time before he understands that it is an advertisement for a flower show. Yes, he can still read. But Crusty's reading is impeded by the informational gap between him and literate society; it takes longer for him to make connections between words and meaning.

Since he no longer functions in the context of information, announcements about the doings of the world take longer to penetrate. It is almost inconceivable to his lethargic mind that there be an event wholly for flowers, a Massachusetts Horticultural

Society that organizes a convention of flowers, in a hall, with a show, and that people spend their time of day looking at nothing but flowers.

It takes even more time for Crusty to relate this event to Spring, but he can see a certain connection, despite being so urban; what interests him really is that there is a place, the Bayside Expo Center, where this happens, and he can get there by subway.

Since it is a large poster, it must be a large event. Mostly Crusty hangs out in the center of town around Copley Square, Tremont Street, Washington Street, Harvard Square, South Station or the North End. That is where the people are. Gathering places are events in Crusty's mind, the focus of people– other special events are the baseball games at Fenway Park and hockey or basketball at the Garden.

In Crusty's equation of the city, where there are people, there is money. The crawling public is his support system. It is like the pigeons who know that where there are people, there are crumbs. Being homeless, no network, means no funds, so being social translates into getting into a crowd. Any crowd. A kind of homing instinct means heading for the action. Home is where the spare change rubs off.

In fact, places of human concourse are a poor man's society– the mall, the subway entrance, the arcade, the train station, the saloon. Somehow, in Crusty's dim mind, Bayside Expo Center sounds like a draw, one of those warm, teeming places, a scene where a few pennies may shake out of the human pocket.

So he takes the rickety Red Line out through South Boston's vacant lots and along the expressway, past the storage warehouses, the Boston Globe, the abandoned light manufacturing, the Amtrak railroad line, out to the desolate U Mass and JFK subway stop, which lets out at the Exit 15 interchange, a car's nightmare, and walks vulnerably along the costly and fancy roads and accesses and roundabout, with the haphazard Boston Skyline stretching out North of here, the untended roadside strips, the neglected botany of the asphalt and concrete sidings, across the enormous parking lot, a wilderness of machines, under the white arches of the Expo Center, to the West Lobby.

It is a world built for the middle-class travelers, and Crusty trudging in on foot is a souvenir from another century, another world, a time when man still walked, when maybe there were still horses, a tramp, a hobo, in his grimy jacket, his scuffed boots.

Hundreds of real, live, affluent people are already thronging lackadaisically to get in, lined up in leisure before the narrow entrance, and Crusty, the street veteran, is very out of place. These people are still warm from their cars. This is not a public place, not in his sense. Legalese aside, a public place to Crusty means somewhere to be inconspicuous. The homeless belong to public places. They are at home, anonymously, where other people feel homeless.

They fit in where anonymity reigns, where the faceless crowd, coming and going, is impromptu, not linear, not individual. Crusty is a sore thumb here, instead, who sticks out at the flower show. These people here for the exhibition are not so finely dressed necessarily, in their outdoor casuals, as if headed out for the woods, or into the garden, plastic jackets, gray-haired women, children, invalids. It is, however, even Crusty notices, some kind of select crowd, an elect of Spring, like at a sporting event but different, coming to see a commercialized Spring, a season preview, a merchandised garden, and Crusty is as out of place as a hard hat at an art show.

But Crusty, for whom the Red Line is a continental journey, has come too far to just turn back. A pigeon's instinct warns him that it is no place for the homeless, that this is a cozy American ritual, but he edges up to the line far back from the official ushers at the entrance and stands there jaw pushed out, hovering in his over-sized parka, a second hand scarecrow, as the people file by, his callused hand out, and he doesn't say a thing. He is only muttering.

That look of suspicion, of cringing, of bother, of irritation that springs up involuntarily in people, that public look of the peace being disturbed, it comes on their faces, just when they are thinking of flowers, of Spring, of the Show, to be suddenly rawly confronted by Crusty, the ravage of a person, a talisman of Winter, a symbol of the great discontent.

51

Willy-nilly it makes people, just his rude being there, aware that the public spends dollars for flowers, not dollars for people, and the sight of him raises that ever lurking specter of private and public guilt.

Crusty, too, knows it is the wrong place for him, he still has a subtle sense of the niceties, he doesn't belong to a festivity, to a world of color, he doesn't belong in normal human cues; the escape routes are not visible here, there is no clutter, no disorganization, no garbage to melt into, but the line is a captive audience and a few stragglers begin coughing up, fumbling in their pockets, as he stands there, a silent cipher of rebuke.

He is a cipher of remorse to their mood of a Spring outing, his mere indelible appearance enough to plead spare change without the words, a few dollars even pass, and one man who sees the disparity of the occasion even gives him a fiver and says, "Enjoy the show."

Crusty doesn't look at them. He doesn't say anything. His incongruity says it all and shortly he has a rumpled fistful of money, society's begrudging ticket to the Flower Show, but it is clear he can't work the line all day.

The space isn't right. The burly parking attendants and the barking ushers will get to him before long so he pockets the cash and wonders what to do. Here he is, flush, but out of place.

Crusty has never been to a Flower show and he is hungry. Maybe inside the big pavilions he can get lost, he thinks, maybe there is even money in there, but the hard, cosmetic, faces of the older women, their pitiless, set hairdos making them look like inert spinsters of middle class order, of some kind of conspiracy of propriety, scares and intimidates him.

This is the kind of people who threaten him most, hardened and impervious though he is to any impression he makes, to the police even, but the very scrubbed decency of them could mean trouble, so he drifts along the ticket line as invisibly, as impersonally as he can. Instinct tells him to go away. It is funny how threatening the middle-age matron of America can be, not even meaning to be, with their plastic fashion glasses, their brittle hairdos, their wrinkled, coiffured, made-up faces and impervious disapproving looks.

Crusty isn't exactly a floral display either, and the ushers notice him too, on guard, nothing here to hide him, no downtown decay to use as camouflage, but there are no cops and he warily holds up the dollar bills and looks at the ground. There is no law against him after all, not yet, and he is in line, he will pay, he isn't loitering.

In the space age it costs eleven dollars to see flowers, though they are free on the Commons, in the public gardens where Crusty spends more time than most citizens. The Department of Public Works doesn't know how often Crusty wanders among the tulips, drawn not because they are beautiful, but because they can't hurt him.

Crusty doesn't actually see flowers the way affluent people do, as signs of cultivation, as tokens of the seasons, as symbols of love, as accents of beauty or color to dapple the mood of the city, to remind the city dweller of the country. Crusty sees the flowers as fellow survivors, as sort of denizens of the privileged pathways, as phalanxes of bright workers employed by the state, by the Municipal Works Department.

To Crusty, they look like some hybrid of social welfare, some form of general relief. They are on a public program, like he is. He does not smell their scent, see their colors, wonder at their form. They are reminders that somewhere in the system there is public spending for things, like flowers. Somehow this is reassuring, but it doesn't occur to him to get sensual pleasure from the floral beds anymore than it does to take responsibility for the programs that keep him alive.

This is something for other people, people with affluent noses and eyes. He is not even thankful. Just accepting.

What strikes Crusty about the flowers is that they are quiet. They don't make noise and they are not in the way. They don't get trampled on. Unconsciously, something about this impresses Crusty and he feels, vaguely, that they are on his side. He admires them because they serve no purpose, like himself.

The pavilions at Bayside Expo, instead, are full of milling people, motivated people, and only gradually does he see into the halls, into the stalls and numbered exhibits, behind the motif in the foyer: a giant, floral, carpeted globe, the world, with continents made of carnations and seas of heather.

The world turns, in all its artifice, like a real world, revolving under strobe light, watered by a spray nozzle, dripping with artificial dew. The floral world is our home, it seems to say, yet Crusty knows better. He looks at it like he would at a puzzle.

Garden centers and horticultural clubs from all over New England have mounted real-life exhibits, bringing in flagstones, benches, gazebos, rocks, fountains, and whole trees.

A real-life pedestrian, that is what Crusty is; it's a long time since he's been to the country. Electric light inside the Expo center supplies a fake sun to this idyllically fake outdoor world, and Crusty moves along smelling pizza from somewhere. The number of cripples enjoying the show is amazing. Crusty feels about cripples the way normal people feel about him. It's not good to be cripple if you live on the streets. You need your legs. One of the sections of the show is for amateurs, mostly potted house plants, and all the stands have awards, blue, red, yellow, or white ribbons.

The judges' plaques say what is good or bad. The three categories are: what is your concept, what is the educational design of the exhibit, and how do you want the viewer to feel coming away from your exhibit. If Crusty were self-conscious, he could learn a thing or two from that. Organic matter is important, as in "good organic matter."

Bemused, Crusty reads with difficulty one of the plaques; he has never gotten a blue ribbon in his life, or any kind of ribbon. He was never in 4-H. Every detail is meticulously organized, incredibly taken care of. Each plant is labeled in Latin and looks like it lives in a home.

In the shelter there are no plants, although Madeleine, the bag lady, told him once that Rosie's, the ladies shelter, puts fresh cut flowers on the tables everyday "to give us the sense of being cared for."

Women have it better than men, Crusty thinks, because society believes that whatever bad happened to the ladies was done to them, while homeless men have done it to themselves.

54

Crusty tends to agree. What he is is his own fault, but he decided that long ago when he gave up on the system; he has forgotten that because it is not useful. But, accepting himself as he is, he is his own man. That's why he's on the streets. Slowly, he comes to a new section of the show called Kaleidoscopes, giant floral arrangements in vases, a professional competition judged on points for design, originality, creativity, texture, organic matter, and labeling. Why didn't they have this stuff in school?

None of it much registers on Crusty, who is still looking for the pizza and beer, but the miniature Japanese gardens catch his bleary eye because people are crowded around peering into the tiny models of shrunken plants, capsules of romance, with baby trees, itty-bitty flowers, doll size fountains and mini-pools filled with slivers of minnows swimming around as if in a real world. In the Orient, Crusty has heard, it's okay to be a beggar– in fact, its a profession.

Fanfare Inc. is running the concession and two black girls, scowling, are serving the slices, both of them tubby as houses, grotesquely round, gigantic, and Crusty notices how many fat people there are walking around. Mostly they are harmless, but they take up so much space, particularly in a shelter– but then there aren't really many fat homeless persons.

Most bums are almost gaunt. He sees the fat people more on malls, at food places, and shopping, not on skid row. But Crusty is aware of them. They also are anomalies. Signs of the culture. The who's who of the streets. He sees them around the subway stops, hanging out. The system produces them too.

Crusty takes his pizza slice and beer and shuffles through the acreage of flowers looking for a place to sit. He sees a uniformed guard and for a moment dully suspects he is being followed, but comes to a white bench on the edge of a replica model farm that is planted with tulips, daffodils, azaleas, and posies against a painted backdrop of fields and blue hills.

Not that it matters to him but it represents Brook Farm, the famous experiment, and he sits down without reading the plaque, which describes the noted community from 1841 to 1847 which once adorned Western Massachusetts as an alternative life style opportunity in the days when the cities were growing, industrialization was burgeoning, and George Ripley, Nathaniel Hawthorne, Thoreau and Ralph Waldo Emerson looked for escape and a transcendental connection to nature.

In fact, Brook Farm wanted to prevent the urban form of life that finally produced Crusty.

Behind Crusty's white bench is a model glass green house representing Brook Farm's pioneering venture into commercial horticulture with herbs, vegetables, and cut flowers for the Boston market.

To Crusty it means nothing more than a place to sit while he munches his pizza, oblivious of the picaresque touch he adds to Brook Farm and the 19th century tableau in which the urban blight that is Crusty's habitat first began to manifest. The past, history, is not part of Crusty's agenda; he even takes the bench, which is part of the exhibit, for granted.

The flower show, instead, is not so bad, he thinks. It's a comfort. His mind even wanders, and suddenly Crusty is thinking about the President, his friend, who so grandly promised change, and was going to focus in on the economy like a laser beam.

Well, now with the scandals the President is going to get his. Some change! Subpoenas, lawyers, special federal investigations, treasury cover-ups, congressional hearings, TV, and oodles of tax money— money for people like Crusty— to track down the paper trail and the operators.

Crusty doesn't care whether the President has done wrong or not, it is just that instead of money for Crusty now everybody has to think about the President and his wife.

The President is Crusty's friend but he should be careful, Crusty muses; with his red nose, his bleary eyes, if they rumpled his hair a bit and one night pushed him out of the Rose Garden, he could easily be homeless too. He almost looks like one of us, Crusty thinks. Without the First Lady, he would be nothing.

Opposite him, Crusty also notices, is a cage of butterflies all lit up with live insects going crazy in the hot lights, hanging upside down from the roof of their pen, darting in and out and fluttering around the glassed-in flowers. There are monarchs, luna moths,

56

and Veronicas looking for a way back to the real sun and bevies of children gather around the exhibit because something is moving. It has a blue ribbon.

Viewers are beginning to look at Crusty too. He seems like part of the show, the gardener, maybe, and a crowd is reading the historical notes of experimental Brook Farm, one of them a well-to-do looking man in a tweed jacket, tweed hat, with a walking stick.

The man is bemusedly considering Crusty, looking him over, a sort of benign curiosity on his face, and Crusty, almost like a reflex, says, "Spare a quarter, mister?"

His voice is hoarse and rough, the man looks slightly surprised, but after a moment fumbles in his pocket and comes up with some spare change. Crusty nods, and the man says, "Have a nice day," but Crusty— is he part of the exhibit— turns to the crowd, mostly of women, and says again, "Spare some change?"

The staid women are shocked but the aura of Brook Farm, the idea of an experimental social life, an exemplary model, with females as equals, is right before them— they have just read it on the placard— and they start opening their purses one by one when the uniformed guard that has been warily following Crusty barges through the crowd and announces, "Okay, Buster, the game is up."

He is a well fed young man, round-jowelled, padded cheeks, baby faced, with crew cut hair and gives a call on his walkie-talkie to security as he takes Crusty by the elbow and the crowd falls back.

Crusty, who hates to be touched, shakes the guard off, and thinks of his secret love, the thing only he knows, his secret weapon. His heartache. His unknown passion.

"Don't give me any trouble, Buster," the guard says, and tries again to grab him by the elbow.

Crusty shakes him off again and stands up. He is onstage and rage is in him, his pizza is not finished, and no one understands his daydream. His secret. He was just beginning to think of *her* on the bench, against the background of Brook Farm, among the flowers. His thoughts had almost turned tender. He had just been about to take out the clipping— her news photograph.

"Oksana," he bellows at the top, of his lungs. "Oksana!"

The guard jerks him and start to move him, pushing, away from the bench.

"Oksana, help!" Crusty cries again. The crowd looks on mystified. No one knows he is in love with the figure skater from far away Russia, the Olympic champion, Oksana Baiul, the sixteen-year old orphan who won at Lillehammer, the slender wraith in the white tutu and blond hair. They are all Nancy Kerrigan people, the local star who placed second. But Crusty first fell in love with the Russian orphan when out of nowhere she won at Prague, and she has been his heartthrob ever since. This is his secret. His daydream. Now he blurts it out.

"Oksana was welcomed at the Marinska Palace," Crusty cries out, as another guard shows up.

The spectators, quiet, look at Crusty pinned by the two guards. He does not struggle. He drags his feet. He shouts, "The mayor of Kiev is going to hear about this!"

"Okay, buddy, quiet does it," the guard says as they hustle him toward the entrance.

"Oksana, Oksana!" Crusty is whimpering now, remembering her on the ice, on the TV in the bar window, where he stood outside in the cold watching her light body twirl, jump, overcoming the tube, the night, the street.

"Oksana will never forgive you!" he tells the guards, remembering her crying after she won the gold, "She's an orphan, she loves flowers."

They have reached the doors and the two guards are forcefully ushering him out, tightly gripping his arms, pushing through the line out to the curb. The gutter. He stumbles down. They give him a shove and one of the guards yells at him, "Go home!"

Crusty straightens up in the gutter. He shakes his jacket out. "Oksana hates you," he hurls back at them. "The mayor of Kiev would never allow this."

"Go home," the guard shouts again, "Or we'll call the police."

They glower at him.

He starts to move. The thing that strikes him about the flower show is that there was no music. It was all silent. Only a few announcements on the public address system: that if you got lost or couldn't find your party to show up at the information desk in the lobby. But otherwise, no music.

In one last glance around, back in the gutter, still thinking of Oksana, he notices something else he should have seen before. Nobody is selling bouquets. A lost opportunity for Madeleine.

On the West End of the Commons between the piano shops, the Steinways, Beauman's, Chickerings, sandwiched in just beyond Pier One imports, is a small obscure pawn shop with second hand items from broken down lands like Russia, Afghanistan, and Mongolia.

No one understands who this shop does business with, why it is locked, or where they get their stock from. Refugees and immigrants must bring in items with them from the homelands, hock them here, and hope to make a little nest egg. Silent, unheard, music haunts the street next door, and a new player piano is even at work in the nearby display window, where its keys eerily play a handless melody that no one ever hears.

Crusty is looking at the handless piano one day that Spring– it seeming to be a picture of his life, keys tapping without a song– and he strolls further along, close to the wall, as always, as if being far from the curb were a protection against some undisclosed occupational hazard, and comes to stop, by chance, in front of the pawn shop. Nothing there interests him. Old icons. New Icons. Pieces of plastic. Books in foreign tongues. Old maps. A samovar. Teacups. A few old swords and daggers. A Swiss knife. A parachute jump suit.

Then he sees the homburg.

It is in the corner, atop a bundle of stacked black clothing, neatly folded, all looking crummy and moth-eaten, dilapidated, shredding, scuffed. There is even a pair of black boots.

The homburg is what catches his eye. Somehow it looks familiar, reassuring, despite being dented, kicked in, broken, worn. He thinks he has seen it before. It reminds him of some thing. A used way of life. Some second-hand memory. Some old newspaper. An old movie. He is bemused.

For a long time he looks at it wondering where he has seen it before and doesn't notice the price tag– 12.50. He doesn't know why he is looking at the Homburg, anymore than he knows why he looks at anything. The days are like this. Wander somewhere. See something. Wonder what it is.

For Crusty, things do not have purpose as for other people. An elevator. For most people the elevator goes up to the office. That makes sense. For Crusty, an elevator might as well be a cloud in the sky. Up and down. It goes nowhere, gets nowhere, does nothing. People get in. People get out. It might as well be a merry-go-round. Elevators are for Lowrys.

But the homburg beckons. It says something. Crusty can't figure out what.

It's not elegance, not the rain, not an evening out, the theater that it reminds him of, but of something else, some dim-witted purpose, something like the piano that plays with no hands, some song on a sound track that is inaudible, some statement that connects to his way of life, who he is, what he is, where he is. Then he sees the price.

He has the new money from the mattress in his pocket. 12.50.

A homburg.

A long process of calculation goes through his lethargic mind and comes out the other end: 12.50.

Somehow that means something. Unlike everything else in the display windows, this not only has some kind of attraction, some meaning, but it's an economic possibility. What do sets of furniture mean to Crusty? Rugs. Lamps. Armani suits. Crockery. Cushions. Everything in the stores is for the home. For Lowry.

If he could believe it, though, the sidewalk is a place to live, furnished with contemporary bedrooms, salons, kitchen suites, and the wardrobe for living there is hanging in front of his eyes. Only glass and money separate Crusty from consumer reality. The street is virtual reality. The shop windows are a looking glass.

His heart skips a beat. Maybe this is for him. He looks around, as is his wont, to see if anybody is watching, if a cop is coming up the street, if some other threat is close at hand, then rings the bell alongside the shop door where it says "by appointment only."

A long wait. Finally, a curved, hunched old lady comes to the door and before she sees Crusty opens the latch a crack and peers out.

"What do you want?"

"The homburg."

She hesitates. Then she opens the door and lets Crusty in. A dummy in armor stands inside the shop, with halberd. There are some old ottomans, saddles, stools, carpets, lanterns. The old woman looks at Crusty with disgust, thinks twice about it, but goes to the window and takes out the homburg, patting it. "Twelve-fifty," she says.

Crusty stares at her. She is holding the hat. With the other hand she reaches for the clothing. "The frock comes with it."

Crusty is dimly aware of how ugly she is. If she's a fairy godmother, there is no mirror in the shop. She looks like Madeleine, but worse, much worse. He hesitates. Then takes the homburg.

It is light. He is surprised. For some reason he expects it to weigh a hundred pounds. Like a helmet. A lead hat. But it is buoyant as a feather. Almost jouncey. He doesn't know what to do, so he tries it on. It settles on his head like a bird. Fits like a glove.

Crusty almost smiles.

The old lady hands him the frock, then the trousers. There is the trace of pinstripes in the dusty clothes, and Crusty is standing there, without a mirror, the homburg on, not knowing where to look.

"Do you want the cane?" the old hag says.

Crusty doesn't know what she means. He is wondering how he looks. It is years since he had a hat, other than his furskin. He can't remember if he ever had a hat.

He takes it off, holds it out, upside down, puts it back on, as if he were practicing. He tries this several times. Each time the hat fits back on perfectly.

Now he imagines himself holding out the hat, quarters falling in like pennies from heaven, the old yellowed silk lining still fraily in place, the hat makers label illegible on the top, the old stitching still holding it together.

"How much is the cane?" he asks. He seems to ask this with a voice almost not his own.

She shows him the cane. It has a pearl tip, an ebony point, a mahogany shine. No curved handle. Somewhere he has seen this cane before too. He is getting older. Sometimes he even hobbles. Maybe a cane would be right. He could lean on it. Walk along, and lean on it. They would think he was cripple. More quarters.

"How much?" he asks.

She shrugs. "The cane comes with the hat," she says.

$12.50. It seems like a bargain. A souvenir of old times.

The thing that tempts Crusty, though, is that he won't look like the other homeless. He hates looking like the other bums. It's as if they all had military uniforms on, a convention: the same haircut, the same beard, the same red eyes, the same crusty skin, the same jackets, trousers, boots. They never change. Day or night.

But with the homburg, the frock, Crusty could be someone. They would notice him. He could go out and beg at night. He would be decent. He would look like somebody. Like Lowry? Even Oksana would notice him.

He reaches in the pocket for the fifty the actress gave him– it is still there. He looks at it, tenderly; he has never seen a fifty. But she takes it from him, goes to the lamp, holds it up against the light.

Two relics, these people, of some untold story, who have never found each other, who even now meet in an atmosphere of pitiless bathos, distrust, and fear. The old shop, looks like an attic of uselessness, the hag like a bird in a cage, a buzzard, and Crusty like a victim of the Great Depression, born too late to catch the benefits of the thirties, of the Great Society, of the New Frontier, as if he had been spit out by a bubble gum machine.

"You want a bag?" she says.

She takes the frock, the rumpled trousers, and behind the counter gets brown paper and wraps his new togs. The package looks greasy, like an old egg sandwich. She still uses string. Hemp. It is frayed at the ends, an odd piece from a collection she has in a counter drawer, and, when she is finished, she hands him the flat package, with the paper stains, and tells him, there are no returnals, to get out and not come back. She doesn't want to see him in her shop again.

A rusty brass bell dingles on the door as he leaves, and Crusty again is out on the street, in the sunshine, with the new frock. Atop the package he carries the homburg and the cane. The only thing he hasn't got are the boots.

Now he has a fresh change of clothes and he wonders where to change. He wants to try the costume out up by the Copley Plaza, near the library, but he doesn't know where to leave his old clothes, so he heads back to the shelter, where he has a locker.

They won't let him in till five o'clock, but that's all right– he wants to try the new costume out after dark anyway, be a night worker, catch the dinner crowd.

He can have the soup at the shelter first, then spend the night out, now that the weather is fine. He'll miss the curfew at the shelter, but it won't matter – he can even take his old jacket in the brown paper along as a cushion, and sleep behind the library on a grate.

He heads back to Pine Street. It is almost five, and the supper crowd is lined up against the wall, hanging there, bedraggled rowdies, down-and-outers from all parts of the city looking like a cue of the unemployed, the ones who never get the job.

Meathead is up front, with several of his cronies, looking for someone to pick on, as usual, and the rest are addicts, disabled veterans, petty criminals, and the mentally deficient, impaired, and ill. There are a few loners, too, like Crusty.

Meathead is trying to set up a game of Boston poker. Once they check in, he scouts the line for a likely candidate, and spots a young newcomer who is a first-timer at the shelter. Meathead befriends him, and his cronies gather around. They are also eyeing Crusty, having spotted his package– the homburg, and the cane.

Boston poker is a four handed card game in which the gull, the newcomer, plays an open hand while the others play a closed hand. The newcomer is required to lay his hand down face up on the table while the others hold their cards. This way they can see what he has. Then the betting begins.

The gull is required to lay all his money on the table. There is no limit. Meathead and his cronies talk a lot and assure the newcomer that there is big money in the game, that he can't lose because he has an open hand, and that everybody new at the shelter has to play.

Of course, in a few hands he is wiped out. Then they extend him credit. He doesn't want to play anymore, but Meathead gives him one look, and the cronies all look alarmed, so the gull runs up an extended bill that he can never pay back and from that time on he belongs to Meathead and the cronies and they tell him where to go, what to do, whom to talk to, and what to say.

Crusty takes a number for his mat, and, choking back a gulp of disgust, goes straight to it and lays out the brown paper package. He hasn't thought this out and now that he sees the homburg, the cane, and the frock on the mat he wonders how he will get it on and out of here without Meathead butting in, or management.

He might put it on in the toilet, or better yet wait till supper, when they are at the soup, and then slip out before they can see him.

He doesn't know exactly what it is he fears, because, as far as he knows, he has a right to wear the frock, homburg, and cane; in fact, he hasn't thought otherwise until seeing Meathead, hasn't thought about the way he would look, or the rules, or anything else except the vague memory of having seen this outfit somewhere before on the street, and it's being the right thing for the night and a few quarters.

On the sly, when Meathead and the others have gone for soup, Crusty sneaks downstairs to the toilets with his package. The shelter is a dormitory style, with plastic paneling and linoleum floors. Everything is the same drab color. It looks like a barracks.

This is where Crusty's dreams, for what they are worth, take place. His dreams mix with the secretions of a hundred other stray

66

men, like anonymous blankets in a central closet, libidos numbered, mats assigned, lockers in a row.

The dreams have no mirrors to play in. Poverty needs no reflection of itself. No pillows to hide under. No upholstery to get caught in. No bureaus to curl up in the top drawer with. No photographs to look at. There is no personality here, no private recess. No place for a dream, unless it is the toilet or under the mat with the boots.

There is nothing left here of Crusty's childhood. No *memento mori*. No relic of a family. No grandfather clock. Nothing feminine either– no dressing table, no lingerie, no bathrobes, no cosmetics, no flowers. This is an operating room for the socially insane. It is culturally antiseptic, worn, cheap. The needs of the street. A few announcements. A few rules.

The only publication is Spare Change, Boston's journal of the streets, by, of, and for the people, and the cover lists Crusty's bill of rights (small caps).

This itself is like a list of absurdities, everything you never wanted to know about being homeless. Because the list is really an anti-list, a bill of grievances.

I HAVE THE RIGHT TO BE TREATED WITH RESPECT.
(Ha ha).
I HAVE THE RIGHT TO SAY NO AND NOT FEEL GUILTY.
(Oh yeah?)
I HAVE THE RIGHT TO EXPERIENCE AND EXPRESS MY FEELINGS.
(Tell that to Meathead.)
I HAVE THE RIGHT TO TAKE TIME FOR MYSELF.
(Who wears a watch?)
I HAVE THE RIGHT TO CHANGE MY MIND.
(A right to a mind?)
I HAVE A RIGHT TO ASK FOR WHAT I WANT.
(Yeah, the stars.)
I HAVE THE RIGHT TO ASK FOR INFORMATION.
(Who says so?)

I HAVE THE RIGHT TO MAKE MISTAKES.
(And take the consequences.)
I HAVE THE RIGHT TO DO LESS THAN I AM
HUMANLY CAPABLE OF.
(I'm not capable of anything.)
I HAVE THE RIGHT TO FEEL GOOD ABOUT
MYSELF.
(Ho ho)

Crusty continues down the stairs into the latrine. This is where he spends some of his best moments in life, behind the toilet door, his pants down, musing on life, on fate, taking a shit. This at least is allowed him.

The shelter has this purpose. Taking a shit in town is a big problem when you own no toilet. Sometimes the whole point of Crusty's morning is going someplace in town where he knows he has access to a toilet. The cafes don't want him. The restaurants won't let him in. A homeless man has to know where every public toilet in the city is. This is his kind of information. Part of the profession.

Crusty gets into the latrine and unfolds the frock and pants. He wishes now he had the black boots. He takes off his togs and clambers into the new dress. No shirt. Just his wool undershirt. The clothes are large. They seem to wrinkle around him as if they hadn't been used for fifty years.

Life seems to be a movie from long ago– the movie hasn't gotten worse, but life has. Reality no longer seems to have the endearing quirks that, when it was still more brutish, it still had. Progress seems to come with sanitization; history does a lobotomy on the scene. The poignancy, the color fade, and modernity simply gets flat, textureless.

Crusty checks himself in the one mirror over the sink. He looks like a figure out of another time, a gilded age, a time when a bum still had his dignity, when a beggar was a cultural landmark, a portrait of humanity. This mirror image, Crusty in the latrine, is now a silhouette of humanity, an aspiration of mankind, an old photo cast aside by the century.

He starts up the stairs. He has his cane. The homburg is in place. The mannequin of poverty, reflecting the dreams of men, about to step out into the night, comes to the top of the flight of stairs and meets Meathead.

Meathead looks him over. He minces this way and that. The cronies gather behind him.

"Charlie," says Meathead, loud and sweet. "Darling Charlie. You're back!"

Crusty tries to push back into the hall.

"Charlie don't recognize his friends, eh? Stepping out? A little date in the limelight?"

Meathead slams him up against the wall. A fist comes down on the homburg.

"Getting too good for the shelter, are we?" says Meathead, and suddenly punches Crusty in the paunch.

Crusty sags.

Meathead takes the cane, knocks the homburg off.

"Well, now, my ass, look at the tramp. All dressed up for malarkey. Shined and spit. Out for a laugh."

Meathead brings the cane down on Crusty's crown. The pearl handled stick breaks. Meathead starts kicking him in the shins. The cronies join in. Crusty slumps to the floor. Meathead shoves him down the stairs. In his frock, Crusty rolls down the steps. His homburg following. Meathead gives it a kick. The hat bounces down the stairs behind Crusty.

"Look at the tramp!" Meathead cries. "Didn't make it up the stairs."

The cronies whoop.

Meathead spits. "Next time you want to laugh at Meathead, just try the homburg."

He looks down in triumph, a Vietnam vet lording it over the past, a homeless leader of the nineties, a bully of the century, spits again, and shouts, "Fuck you, Charlie."

Still the tulips in the Commons are blooming. Giant and red, they cup the air, hundreds of them, erect as sentinels of Spring. Real Spring - not the Flower Show.

Crusty ambles along, after the long walk from the old armory, and feels buoyed up by the blooms, as if for a moment here were somewhere else– Holland, perhaps, not at the flower show anymore.

Even he is allowed to enjoy these flowers and forget for a moment that the municipality has put them here, no doubt for some reason. The bulbs of yesteryear.

If he were a normal citizen, if he didn't have to exercise extra caution in public places, if he didn't know that some of these strollers were actually city agents or even policemen in disguise, he would pick a few flowers for Madeleine, the bag lady, who is probably over behind the statue, on her usual bench.

There she is. They call this section of the Commons the Public Garden, at the foot of Commonwealth Avenue, with its replicas of the gaslights. Crusty, despite himself, smiles.

It is because he sees himself spoiling the movie that might be going on right here at the hub of the Eastern United States, on this fine Spring day. All these chic people living in the luxury of the bottom of the avenue, shoed into their elegant cement boxes, attended by the liveried doormen of Brahmin city, hailing taxicabs from under the green, canopied entrances of the urban high life. If only the actress stays home, he thinks.

The actress has come into Crusty's life by surprise. Madeleine knows nothing more about her than about Oksana. He was panhandling at the entrance to the park when she came by with her dog.

He could tell by the way she walks she is someone, and the dog itself has an aloof, disdainful, mysterious air about it. She has on a hat that no one in regular life wears and it is clear that she does not belong to humdrum existence the way a normal person does.

A normal person looks worse than the surroundings, especially in the park, but the actress is as if on the lookout for something, and herself seems to be in a costume play as if the rest of the world should be a theater in which she can star.

Thus she looks better than the world around her, the Eastbound traffic, the dirty cabs, the unwashed cars, the trash bins, the stone walls, the drab trees. Her dog senses this and is on the lookout for a hydrant, a tree, or a hub cap to be discreet on, when he smells Crusty.

As the dog pulls the leash, she takes no notice, thinking the beastie has chosen an appropriate place, and absentmindedly lets him tug her along to the very spot where Crusty is holding out his hand.

She does not even notice as the dog sniffs Crusty's boots, assuming he is a wire trash basket maybe to pee on or some other refuse that has been left there by the Department of Public Works, until the dog begins to whimper. Instead of doing its duty, it sits back on its haunches and looks up at Crusty, panting, waiting to be petted.

Crusty is at a total loss. If he pets the dog, the lady might be offended, maybe even call the police. If he moves, the dog may bite him. If he speaks to the lady she might be insulted, might hit him with her handbag.

He isn't supposed to be at the entrance to the park anyway, so he just stands there like a statue. A living statue, not far from the equestrian bronze of Washington at the bottom of the great avenue and the other pieces of marble and statuary that garland the place.

Besides, the lady looks perplexed when she does notice what he is, but there is very little she can do about it, because the dog begins to lick Crusty's boot.

Crusty just stands there.

He is pretty sure this is going to lead to trouble. Some of the boys down at the shelter would just kick the dog and move on, but Crusty likes the actress, and doesn't want to harm her dog. So he just stands there waiting for the axe to fall, not looking at her, and letting the dog lick him.

He is pretty sure that Madeleine would be jealous if he told her about this, because Madeleine, warts and all, thinks she is the only lady in his life. She doesn't even know about Oksana, his secret. After all, this is her beat, whereas he has no right to be here, except sometimes to meet Madeleine or have a pretzel.

The dog just keeps on licking. When he has cleaned one boot he begins on the other. Crusty is close enough to the actress to see the color of her eyes, but she doesn't pull the leash, or look at him, but just waits patiently to see what will happen.

The dog finishes licking Crusty's boots, then sits back on his haunches again, looking up with big brown eyes full of admiration, as if Crusty were a revered master.

This puzzles Crusty, but the actress says, "Dogs always recognize good people."

He hasn't told Madeleine about it. He wouldn't now. Somehow it is a secret between him and the dog that the actress called Gypsy. She gave him a command and he backed off, straining at the leash, eager to be off. The actress looked at Crusty, followed the dog, and smiled.

It was a wan smile. As if the world were lost, and going to hell, and only the dog knew where to go. Departing, she even looked as if she wanted to stay, maybe to chat a little. But the dog had other purposes and she was its mistress.

She had given the startled Crusty fifty dollars.

Today Madeleine is in her usual togs. He ambles up, feet slightly apart, toes slightly out, scuffling slowly, making very little progress, as if there is a lot of ground to cover, lingering where he is, as if it is better there, and to really arrive would maybe be a disaster.

Madeleine pays no attention to him as he shuffles in, her eyes on the outlook for pigeons, or smaller birds, her leggings drooping down around the ankles, the ankles swollen, winter or summer, a sort of leather, slipper-like galosh fringed with rabbit fur on which serves either as a boot or a slipper, a wire-mesh dolly with three wheels beside her, filled with packages wrapped in plastic, the whole thing looking dirty and unappetizing.

No purse. No handbag. Everything is in the dolly. She is frowning. Maybe it is the sunlight. Her coat is a sort of indoor-outdoor housecoat, a bathrobe, looks twenty years old, and is tattered in one shoulder.

He sits down in a heavy, resigned way, as if a stone landed on the bench. She is staring straight ahead.

Crusty wonders what is for lunch. He stares straight ahead too. The two of them are four eyes in rags staring straight ahead, seeing nothing, saying nothing, not even thinking anything. Except lunch. And the birds.

People passing by might think they have been sitting there forever, the two of them as if they have born this way. They might wonder what their names were, where they had come from, how they got this way, why they didn't go somewhere else.

Years might pass. The passersby might return, and there they would be still, the same as ever, nothing changed, nothing bettered, all the same. They might remember having seen them before, on the same bench, just sitting there, staring straight ahead, not even holding hands.

Someone might return, remembering a flower, a lover, something good, and find these two people sitting on their bench, where that memory was, and they would not be able to sit there because these two were there, in the way, taking the space. Defining the moment forever.

It is as if the gardeners came and went, the flowers bloomed and withered, the municipal truck collected the trash– yet, still, there they are. People pass by thinking it should not be allowed, that

74

something should be done about them, that it is an outrage, a pity, illegal, anything. But there is not anything. Just the two of them. Looking that way. Being that way. In plain daylight. In the big city. In the middle of the park.

Crusty thinks of the actress. Madeleine continues to stare straight ahead, as if immune to his thoughts. Usually she reads everything in his mind. Not this time. Fifty dollars is a lot of money. If he were fair about it, he would give Madeleine ten. After all, she feeds him. To Crusty, who averages around 4.50 a day, when he is in a good spot, it means almost ten days savings.

On the other hand, he would like to take Madeleine to a big meal, down on the harbor, at Jasper's, and they could watch the valet park the town cars and limousines, peek up at the stars, walk along the waterfront and see the light rippling on the waves, hear the lapping of the sea on the shore's granite rocks, and kiss in the moonlight. All for twenty-five dollars apiece.

He has forgotten the rats. The stench. The parked cars. The racket. The fact that Jasper's costs around $75 a head with the wine, that Madeleine has nothing to wear, the warts, the lack of any place to sleep, that to dine at Jasper's you probably need your social security card, your draft card, your passport, your license, your credit cards, your checkbook, your city ID, you Xpress 24 hour card, and your latchkey.

The idyll on the bench, and fifty dollars in his pocket, the actress, and above all the dog, Gypsy, that look in the dog's eyes after he licked Crusty's boots, all this has enchanted Crusty's dull mind for a moment and he is dreaming of the wedding bells at the Pilot House, the priest, the black frock, and Madeleine, pretty as a dog, all dressed in ribbons, spangles, lace, veils, and frumpery, edging towards him and saying, in a far away voice, that drifts out of the midnight moon like a song, "I do."

All for fifty dollars. The night in the hotel included. And a trip to Niagara.

Madeleine, of course, is not entirely oblivious to all this– it is her dream– but does not know that she is transformed from brown woolen hanging drawers, straggling hair, broken teeth, tattered togs, and galoshes into the princess of the night, that she is dining at

Jaspers, that Crusty has asked her to marry him– no, that she is marrying him in a gala harbor-side romance without his even ever having to ask.

Thus he is thinking his thoughts. She hers. They might sit this way forever, but she speaks.

"Do you want me to do you now, or after lunch?"

Back to reality. The dream seems more real to Crusty, when his mind, from its lethargy, from it deadened memory, lights up and he has fifty dollars, the dog, and dinner at Jasper's. Even the actress is there. All this seems more real than 4.50 a day, and Madeleine, with her raspy voice, actually speaking to him.

He doesn't answer. He prefers to be done before lunch, because then he can recover while he is eating. It doesn't pay to be debonair. Even so, he wishes Madeleine could be more romantic about it, not that she isn't skillful, but it sounds so matter of fact. He remembers the dog licking his boots. Even the actress. Her bonnet.

"Well, do you?"

He supposes so. He knows of course Madeleine wants to marry him. Not at Jaspers. For real. She has even proposed to him.

"Crusty," she said, "we don't need to live on the street. We could have a home."

That was how she began. Crusty asked her what she meant. "We could be together," she said, "in a home. Like man and wife. A woman needs security."

"No money," said Crusty.

"Money's not everything," said Madeleine. "We could tell the Urban Redevelopment and Placeless Authority Administration that we are getting married. They respect that. It means two rooms instead of one. Sometimes there is even a little kitchen. I could cook for you."

He remembers this scene, even as she starts fumbling around with his zipper. These pants are not ideal. Twice as much stuff as normal pants. Double layers. But they're warm.

"Rent," he thinks he answered her.

"I could pay the rent," she said.

"We're getting too old for that," Crusty told her.

"We could have a bed, Crusty," she said to him. "I wouldn't have to do you in the park."

She already has his zipper open.

For some years, before he got involved with this bag lady, he had been celibate. He thought it was part of being on the street. Then he met Madeleine. The first time she offered him lunch in the park, she said, "Why don't you do yourself?" Being celibate had had its advantages. He had to worry about the police less. He didn't have to worry about messing in the shelter. He had no woman to worry about. No home. No bed. No rent. No dirty underpants.

The other men didn't bother him. He wasn't as worried how he looked, or if he was acting alright, if he was doing something wrong, bothering somebody, making his mother sick, if his prostate was okay, if he had Aids, or where to find the next woman.

There was a certain stability and peace to being celibate, but the social worker kept insinuating that he was missing out on a pleasure. The joke was that even when he was celibate, Crusty wondered what it would be like to take a roll with her in the basement of the shelter.

Madeleine is no social worker but the homeless are not allowed to fraternize with homeful people, the social worker included, so a bag lady is about all that is available. Not that he went looking for Madeleine.

She had been selling flowers that day. Roses. She invested in the roses at a floral wholesaler, wilted, of course, freshened them with a little water, but they were drab anyway. She was at a corner near the Copley looking as pretty as possible, with these pathetic roses for sale.

Nobody was buying. So Crusty, out of some impulse that he didn't understand, took a spot near her against the wall, and held out his hand. People began buying the roses. Pretty soon Madeleine was sold out.

She had rolled up her rags, packed the cart, and as she pushed by him she said, "Follow me."

They traipsed across the West End to the park, where after nosing around the benches, Madeleine plumped herself down on the slats of one of the worst benches, the one they are on now, near an overflowing trash bin, and patted the seat next to her.

Crusty sat down. It was like the end of a long journey. She got out the baloney sandwiches, and two bottles of beer, rummaging in her cart among jars of peanut butter, jelly, old butter, stale bread, heads of rotten lettuce, ends of cheese, soft tomatoes, laundry, and a few knick-knacks, and said, "Why don't you do yourself? Or do you want me to do you?"

Crusty was pretty surprised. Now again her hand is firmly in place, inside the zipper, without any exposure, no indecency, but Crusty doesn't know where to rest his eyes. He looks straight ahead, thinking of the actress; a woman with a stroller pushes by right in front of them, the grounds keeper is not far away, sticking the litter with his pickup, jabbing it into a roll-along can, and Crusty can see the equestrian statue of Washington riding Eastwards, monumental, proud, overcoming.

His eyes begin to blur slightly and he begins to think, not only of Oksana, and the actress, but, for some reason— of Greece.

part two

It is nearly thirty years earlier.

Crusty, a young man, is in Piraeus, the port of Athens. He has some other name. It is not a Greek name, though– an ordinary name that no one would remember, like Jones, an American name, an everyday name. Perhaps it is of no importance. Even sitting on a park bench today, wrapped in the present, Crusty himself no longer remembers the name he had then. Names belong to rich people. Biographies are like personal property. Crusty is dispossessed of all that. But he had a private name then: and he was in Greece.

It is a long time ago, many a day back, many a meal before, and everything is under a dismal haze of lost memory.

The blue bay of Athens' port is studded with white boats, the low silhouette of land stretching left and running into the harbor and land on the right, is slightly opaque today, as if the fish had gone somewhere else. Industry pockmarks the land in this country of temples, and the sun is skrimmed behind a shawl of white smog. It must be Spring. He is standing on a pier.

The cement is bare of sailors. No palms. No cypress. No cedar here. Some longshoremen are working the next wharf, and Crusty is with someone– he can't remember who. Some stray hawsers line the pier, some cars from the city are parked nearby, and a taxi. A stray butterfly or two, bleached, as if from inland, are fluttering about, entirely out of place, and parched grass grows from between the cracks. The water near the pier is darker, and Crusty is peering into his future and cannot see anything.

Nobody is fishing. Some bags of hemp are stacked up to the side of the pier, and there are some rubber tires lying about. No birds today. The clouds are cumulus, small, fuzzy, diffracting light. Something is wrong. Something is berserk.

Crusty, or whoever he was then, can feel it. An ominous presence as if he is being watched. Nervously he scratches himself as if mosquitoes were biting him, but there are no mosquitoes. The Greek government cleared them from the harbor long ago before the war. It looks like there might be rats here, but he is not looking for them. The taxi bothers, as if he should be going someplace, but doesn't know where. Up to Athens?

He should make a telephone call. But what is the number? Whomever he is supposed to call was just with him, he thought, or is he supposed to have lunch with her? He wishes he could shake off this sense of surveillance, and wonders why they came down to the harbor anyway. There must have been something to look at, or was it simply for the food. Or were they on a trip?

He must be lost. She isn't here. Maybe she went to the toilet. That's the first place she heads for in any establishment. Perhaps she is in one of the cafes. That's where he will go. He will find her.

He takes a deep breath, looks up, and there is the vessel. A monolith. Sixty thousand tons at least, and painted black with white superstructure.

Panic. Startlement. Almost bewilderment. How could he not have noticed the giant liner before, there, just to his right, still in the harbor, black from the waterline up. White above, nose into the harbor, awesome bridgework, decks empty, scores of portholes peering shorewards. A handsome vessel.

Bemusement. She, the boat, seems almost like a ghost ship at this Greek port of call, perhaps in quarantine. Nobody is boarding; nobody is disembarking. The imposing gangplank, unguarded, beckons to shore, canopied, slanting upwards into the big ship's belly. Crusty shivers.

Where is such a liner over here from? She almost looks like a prewar vessel.

He looks her over from bow to stern– transfixed. Suddenly, from her shapely stern she is flying the sinister red flag– hammer and sickle. Crusty shudders.

Now she looms up, gigantically, iron and steel, immensely silent, and involuntarily his frightened eyes scan slowly to the bridge, where lone and uniformed, crisp and tall, shoulders above the guard rail, white hat on, the officer of the day is regarding him, Crusty, through a large pair of menacing binoculars.

Crusty observed immediately feels smaller, as if he is being sucked into the eyeglasses, self-conscious of being an American. An imperialist. The binoculars seem to threaten his existence; they are inquisitive as to what he is doing in Athens. What right he has to be in Piraeus? Why he is standing on the dock, alone, not fishing, not toting hemp, not driving a taxi, not sweeping the wharf. In a word, why isn't he working? A laborer. Who does he think he is?

Crusty, in the grimness of the Cold War, is deeply disturbed. He wishes he were on the bridge, looking down. He has a sudden, overweening, irrational wish to be Russian himself with a berth of his own, visiting Athens, with shore leave, headed back up the Bosporus into the Black Sea for some mysterious home. The motherland. To build socialism! He swallows hard.

What if he moves? He has been standing here seconds, minutes. The binoculars are still on him, and he strains forward to see who it is that is looking at him. He is being hypnotized by the binoculars.

He must move. Yes, whomever he is with may in this minute be looking for him. He must go to the café.

He forces himself. But as he crosses the pier to the harbor square he feels the binoculars still following him, till he gets to the Doxos, with its white tables spilling out onto the cobblestones, its blue awnings– but she isn't there. Only a few early morning customers are about, and the waiter in black trousers, white blouse, and a tray in his hand.

Crusty, under the surveillance of the Russian ship, pretends to be in control and sits down. It is years, and era ago. He is still a young man. He is still smoking. This was when he still bought cigarettes. Except for smoking, he may even be a beautiful young man, though he admires the Greek waiter who has good looks to burn. Panache. Street smarts. Creased pants. Shiny shoes. A job. Doesn't even need a visa to live in Greece. Still, Crusty is thinking about the boat. The vessel. The Soviet Union.

He orders a coffee, Greek style, and pays in drachmas. The coffee is like Turkish, but Turkish here is a dirty word. He feels like a Turk himself. He is calculating the distance to the gangplank.

He can't be sure, really, whether the waiter is sneering at him or smiling. The binoculars are still on him. The coffee is sticky sweet. He imagines, for a minute, being the waiter serving a Turkish tourist, then remembers the boat, and Crusty wonders, in panic, if he has his ticket home, wherever that is, or whether he is a Turk immigrating to Georgia, where Stalin was born, where the fruit trees grow in abundance, the hills are ripe with wheat and grain, Yalta, where the Russians themselves vacation and are even occasionally seen in swimming suits. The boat beckons. The whistle is about to blow.

Sipping Greek coffee, he dreams of it all. If only she were here, his wife, yes, his wife– at least he thinks she is his wife– his girl, he could talk it over with her. After all, it is a big step. Maybe they could even go together, if it weren't for the children they left behind– somewhere; she also has her ticket back, whatever else she is doing, probably right on this square. Maybe the waiter knows where she is. But he can't ask. The waiter would think he was crazy. The boat seems to be impatient, about to sail. The binoculars are still piercing him.

Again he is trying not to smoke. Actually, it is for her sake. He would even give up a cigarette for her. Of course, she is not looking just now, but she might turn up at any minute.

He remembers walking his son somewhere, the little boy perched on his shoulder, and there is a garden, a sunny day, and he is smoking a cigarette, glad of the fresh air, happy to be with his son, when suddenly the gardener straightens up from a row of beets, comes over, smiles, and offers the baby child a cigarette. Oh. How he doesn't want his son to smoke. He remembers that. The moral of the garden.

Besides, the deck officer on the boat can still see him. What else has he done wrong? What else has he to hide? People, moreover, are beginning to turn out. A busload of tourists arrives. Some birds flutter into the square, seagulls, terns, or pigeons— or are they doves? It's hard to tell. They're Greek.

Maybe the boat is leaving. Maybe it is already too late to catch the future.

Crusty leaves a tip. The binoculars on the bridge are still on him, so he cuts across the square, weaving an arabesque, heading for the building on the corner where he can take cover. If he walks a crooked path it will be harder to see where he is going. The guns of the Cold War are invisible. But they are everywhere. The customs building will provide some shade if he has to stay here all day, and block the vision from the boat. He will be able to think.

When he gets to the corner, he stops and leans against the wall. The square is livening up. Here he has his peace, for a moment, and he could light up. But he won't. He will be true to her. The trouble is, his next thought is the big boat, the Dardanelles, the open sea beyond, and the tempting gangplank leading from here— to Georgia!

Crusty looks suspiciously around. If he stands here too long the customs officials will wonder what he is doing. They will ask him for his passport. Ask him what his name is. Where he comes from. How much money he has on him. If he is alone. Is he alone? Maybe she won't come back. Maybe she is with the Greek waiter. Maybe Crusty himself is a smuggler.

He edges away from the wall. Trying to project confidence, he executes another arabesque, drifting toward the wharf, approaching the gangplank. No one is standing guard. He is going to leave the West. Say goodbye to all that. He looks belatedly around, raises his foot, and accesses the gangplank, climbing the ramp, as in a photograph. It is as in a movie.

The next thing that happens is that he is asking for political asylum. The binoculars.

"What's your name?"

87

No answer.

"Where do you come from?"

No answer.

"Are you with someone?"

He wonders where she is.

At this moment, she is at the telephone on the square, with the Greek waiter, who is lusting for her but, because he is well bred, and professional, has shown her where the phone is and said that he saw a man much like her description, served him a coffee, and saw him act suspiciously, crossing the square in a strange manner, hide behind the customs building, and then head for the Russian boat.

"Police!" she hears them reply on the phone.

She has been trained to give the police as little information as possible, because she is German. The ways of the war. A daughter of the war. Don't speak to the authorities. It all seems like a long time ago.

"What do you want?" they ask her.

She hesitates. "To report a missing person," she says. "An American...."

In Moscow, Crusty is placed under observation at the Botkin Hospital, locked ward, for Russians– the mental ward, although the hospital has very good doctors, and treats foreigners, even diplomats. Ludmilla, an English speaking Intourist interpreter whose usual beat is the Berlin Hotel, but who has connections to the "organs"– KGB and MVD, is assigned to his case.

KGB opens his file, upon referral from the Passport Office, and Crusty is code named: Gogolnik– partly because of his overcoat.

A cold irony of the war system is that if you defect– that is, if you believe the Red propaganda of the Soviets, far from being treated as a Hero of the Republic, you are under suspicion of being a lunatic. The Soviets spend billions of rubles to convince the world of the future of Socialism, and then, when Crusty defects, hypnotized by the binoculars, he is immediately treated as a crazy man. A suspect of the People of the People of the Revolution. A madman. And committed for observation to the Botkin closed ward mental department in Moscow, this flat city of Northern Muscovite grays and colossal buildings.

This is Ludmilla's first American case. She is very patriotic. When Crusty says, "I want to be a worker," she beams.

She is very curious. "Do you have cows in America?" she asks. "Do you have pigs?" She tells him the Russian names for these,

and makes animal noises. They laugh. Crusty likes Ludmilla. She
has long pretty ears.

"I want to belong to the party," Crusty tells her.

"Good," she says. "But that can wait. First we have to write to
the Supreme Soviet and say you want to stay in Russia."

"Yes," says Crusty. "I want to stay in Russia. There is no
unemployment, no hunger, no taxes in Russia. No unhappiness. I
want to build Socialism."

"But to build socialism you have to work," says Ludmilla. "If
you do not want to work it is not taken as a contribution to this
country. To work, you have to be able to do something."

Crusty looks crestfallen. "Even in a factory?" he pleads with
her. "There must be a job in a factory where I don't know how to do
anything."

He is already half in love with Ludmilla, his Kremlin gal, with
her long ears, and he is hatching a plan, maybe– if she marries him,
although she is really just a peasant girl, he will be able to stay in
the Soviet Union. Even though they are watching, he tries to kiss
her– but gently, asking first.

"No," says Ludmilla, "it is against the rules. In Russia girls
marry first and kiss later. I would lose my job if I kissed you. You
are American. No, no, later maybe. Now in the letter you must say
why you want to stay in Russia."

"To kiss Ludmilla," Crusty says.

"No, no. This is Socialism."

"My country is in favor of war," says Crusty. "I cannot go back.
They would shoot me. Besides, in Russia, you have soul. I want to
have a soul."

Ludmilla puts down her pen. "That is not a reason," she says.
"This letter is to the Supreme Soviet. They will ask: why? Did you
kill someone? Steal? This is what they want to know."

"I want to read Marxist-Leninist literature," says Crusty. "I
want to be free."

"Do you want to build the State?"

"Oh yes. Of course," says Crusty, looking at Ludmilla's lips.

She smiles. "That is good," she tells him. "They will believe
that."

"Communism is so sexy," says Crusty. "Everybody comrade."

"There are regulations," answers Ludmilla. "We have regulations for those things. Girls do not just kiss. We are interested in the future."

But when Crusty's letter goes up to the Supreme Soviet, and the boss of OVIR– secretary of passports, Alexander Bombachov, even calls to the KGB officer, Guselkov, and urges him, saying, "We ought really to do something on Gogolnik's behalf," Guselkov answers:

"Why?"

It does not matter that Crusty has defected, that he has asked for asylum, that he wants to be Russian, to be Soviet– it does not matter that since 1917 the State has been promoting and propagandizing for this all around the world. No. It does not matter that Crusty is a casualty of the Cold War, that his ego is a lost pawn in the game of political chess between Moscow and Washington. When officialdom hears of it, and hears that they should do something about Crusty, they merely say, "Why?"

Not only. Personally, Guselkov hates a traitor. In the Soviet Union, treason is the highest crime. No matter that all the machinations of the State work tirelessly to win over the hearts and minds of people like Crusty– it is a hollow victory.

Guselkov detests the actual deed, the unpatriotic rejection of motherland, any motherland. There is no pity even. Merely an embarrassing scorn, as if they were women who had been cheaply seduced.

Defectors, after all, after the brief glory of the seduction itself, are in fact scum– worse than dissidents, psychotics, addicts, criminals. To Guselkov a traitor to his country is some kind of an insect, a bug. Why has Marxism-Leninism not foreseen that? Why should he, Guselkov, a Colonel, have to lift a finger for this Gogolnik?

Finally, Crusty is released from the Botkin Hospital and given a small room on the 4th floor of the Metropole Hotel, the floor where the hotel help sleep. It is about big enough for Crusty and his overcoat; not even Ludmilla will come to the room. No telephone.

No bath. No TV. Ludmilla has no good news. Crusty is in a state of limbo. He is under surveillance.

From the KGB file:

Surveillance performed from 08:00 to 24:00 on Jan. 10:
At 11 o'clock, Gogolnik left Hotel Metropole and went to GUM. There he came up to the candy department and asked a salesperson some questions, then took money out of his pocket and went to a cashier of this department. He did not pay for anything but just put the money back into his pocket and started pacing fast on the floor of the department store up and down looking at different goods. Then he went back to the candy department, paid three rubles for an ice cream cone, began licking it, went up the second floor. There he spent some time in the department of ready-made clothes, looked through available suits, then left GUM store walking fast. He was back in his hotel by 11:25.
At 12:45, he came out of his hotel room and went to restaurant. He took a seat at vacant table and began to eat. (No observation was made during the meal because no other people were in there).
At 13:35 Gogolnik left restaurant and went back to his room.
At 18:10 he left his room and went to restaurant. He took vacant table, had his meal, left restaurant at 18:45, and took elevator to fourth floor where he went to his room.
He did not leave his room up to 24:00 after which time no observation was made till morning.

An opaque report, but Ludmilla, in her stolid way, tries to be encouraging as Crusty waits for residential papers. "There is an opinion," she says in officialese, "which exists that you should buy a new overcoat." But Ludmilla never eats with Crusty; she doesn't have the money. Neither does he. But they give him coupons for his food.

The question, at the highest levels, since Crusty could, after all, by a spy, is what to do with a person, unknown to those involved– a person, moreover, who would be a future American bum.

The case against Crusty would, in Yaroslavl, where he was to be shipped, be eventually developed, of course, because you cannot have an American without having a spy, so the organs must develop the case against the spy– in fact, develop the spy. Crusty has a new resumé.

Thus in Yaroslavl, when Crusty is shipped there, a city Northeast of Moscow, much to his own disappointment, since he hoped to stay in Moscow– Igor Padronich, who had been sent to Yaroslavl to "strengthen the cadres" and who was Deputy Chief of Branch for Counterintelligence, assigns Alexei Slyevich as Crusty's developer– a bureaucratic role in which the developer is appointed to fatten the file and make a case against the suspect.

This includes a lot of surveillance and analysis, for instance, how does the subject learn Russian– if he learns too fast it is a sign that he has previous knowledge, and if he learns too slow it is a sign he is covering up. All contacts are inspected minutely.

Any signs of interest in military sites and off bounds are regarded with keen interest. Interest in radio equipment is an alarm signal. Signs of coded messages or semiotic systems, clippings from newspapers, invisible ink are all carefully monitored. Alas Gogolnik shows none of the agent's characteristics, indeed, seems utterly boring and unsuspicious, eats, sleeps, and talks ... only to pigeons!

His only complaint is the cold. It is always chilly. His feet are numb. But Ludmilla says, "Well, you came to this society to build Socialism, so you don't have to feel cold; you should feel proud!"

Before leaving Moscow, Crusty buys a new pair of shoes. He gives his old shoes to Ludmilla. "You want a gift?" he says. "The shoes are my gift to you so that you will know what kind of worn out shoes Americans wear."

"We don't need gifts like that," answers Ludmilla. "We've been wearing worn out clothes all our lives. It's nothing new for us."

The Russian organs, in all their arrogant, pompous efficiency, are dealing with a future bum. The prospect, because they do not know the future, despite communism, is very threatening. In the communist system, what might happen is more suspicious than what does happen. But the bureaucratic system has no control for this. It is established to generate suspicion. So Crusty's frequent trip to GUM, the department store, are analyzed with rare professionalism. Most suspect is the fact that he seldom buys anything.

This is not attributed to his having no money, as it might have been in a capitalist society, or to the foresight that Crusty would one day be a bum, but to a suspect attitude toward Russian consumerism, as if Crusty were going to report on the price of perfume, the availability of soap, the popularity of black underpants. Alexei spends considerable time working up this aspect of the case and it even comes to the attention of Guselkov.

The two of the discuss the matter at headquarters:

Guselkov: "He does not eat enough beets."

Alexei: "Or potatoes."

Guselkov: "There is an opinion which exists that Gogolnik wants to kiss Comrade Ludmilla."

Alexei: "This is true."

Guselkov: "Why?"

Alexei: "Perhaps he has a motive."

Guselkov: "Precisely. Ahem…"

Alexei: "Yes sir?"

Guselkov: "The system does not allow kissing."

Alexei: "No sir."

Guselkov: "We both believe in the system."

Alexei: "Yessir."

Guselkov: "You have spoken to Comrade Ludmilla?"

Alexei: "Yessir."

Guselkov: "She believes in the system too?"

Alexei: "Yessir."

Guselkov: (twirling a paper opener) "Very suspicious!"

At his bench in the Yaroslvl Plastics Works, Crusty is a checker of components, a regulator, and he has about three feet of space, a small lamp, and is one of several hundred workers in the wing.

The components are exuded plastics, and Crusty has no idea what they are for– TV, radios, missiles; he has several samples on his bench and all the rest have to be exactly the same, without defects, ticketed with an examiner's number, matched up against a mould, fitted with screws, and then sent to the packers on a tray. Crusty is a Soviet worker.

The Yaroslavl Plastic Works is a large factory about a quarter of a mile long by an eight of a mile wide, a sprawl of streets and sheds, three or four main buildings, alleys, vans, and trucks. Crusty wears a white gown and kerchief and makes a regulator 1st grade in the plant not far from Krasnava Illitsa, or Red Street, and the Volodaskogo tram stop.

His wage is 700 old rubles a month, quite good by some standards, but he receives a bonus of 700 rubles a month from the Russian Red Cross, which he gets as a defector and ward of the State.

The organs want to be very careful about Crusty because as an American he is probably a spy, yet Guselkov and company also realize there is a chance that Crusty is a humanitarian case and they want to give him his chance to be a good Soviet citizen. He is given a small but desirable apartment down on the river with a view, and it only costs him eight rubles a month.

It is not long before Alexei notices and reports that Crusty seems to be singularly lacking in any grasp of ideological dialectics and has no talent for Marxist-Leninist doctrine– on the other hand, there is an opinion that this is a ruse or cover-up on the American's part and that he is hiding a much deeper knowledge of the Soviet System than shows on the surface.

He is soon drawn into a fight on his third day by a trouble maker, Victor Pobedy, who makes rude insulting remarks in English about American pigs at Crusty's bench, but colleagues separate them quickly before Victor can thrash poor Crusty, who is no match for the Russian.

The foreman, who has been assigned to teach Crusty a little Russian, takes them both into his office and says, "You are equal. He's an American. You are a Russian. But you are both workers."

Crusty is not much interested in labor or production– it just doesn't come naturally to him, and it is not long before he notices signs of the kind of society he is in: mass gymnastics, compulsory after work meetings with a political agenda, compulsory lecture attendance, and compulsory participation in the potato harvest on Saturdays and Sundays as a patriotic duty. People also look strangely at him when he listens to the radio.

Dimitri, the foreman, gives Crusty Russian lessons in a second-floor room, sometimes before work, sometimes after work; Alexei has instructed Dimitri, "Don't discuss anything about his life before he came here." As a result, there is no personal discussion. Just verbs, and a little colloquial Russian.

Crusty is not suspicious, but reserved, if anything lethargic, but he thanks Dimitri for his lessons. It doesn't matter. Dimitri doesn't like him. As a person of the old school, Dimitri thinks nobody could be worse than a traitor. A man untrue to one side will always betray the other too. It is an official assignment, however, and he never lets Crusty know. The fact is, even Crusty is more likeable than Dimitri.

Crusty once has this conversation with the foreman.

> Dimitri: *"How is it that you are once again remiss in work, comrade?"*
>
> Crusty: *"What about the Russian soul?"*
>
> Dimitri: *"You mean vodka? Ha ha!"*

Their conversations are always short. But Shuskevitch, who works on a nearby bench, likes American cigarettes too, when Crusty can get them, which is not often, and they get off the detail and smoke outside the shop.

Shuskevitch will say: "Dimitri is not really a new man."

"You are my friend," Crusty will say, "you have a soul."

Then Shuskevitch will say, "Vodka. Ha ha."

The only thing that Crusty really seems interested in, besides shopping, is the girls— whether they are workers at the other benches or show up at the Trade Union Hall dances. Being American, Crusty is something of a novelty and even on the factory floor when he passes their benches girls he doesn't know will say, "Hi!"

From the KGB file, March 16:

> *Informant has noticed nothing suspicious about Gogolnik's behaviour. Almost never talks about life in his country, and never about how he got here. Will exchange a few words with boys or girls at lunch break, but in these situations he speaks positively about technology and position of workers in USSR.*
>
> *He is not a worker. He treats his job not well. He shows no interest, and his behaviour and attitude towards work causes complaints from other workers. He is lackadaisical.*
>
> *This may all be a pretense. There are two opposed hypotheses. Either Gogolnik is part of a foreign intelligence plan, or he is not but has some psychological difficulty. We are observing whether he tries to cultivate Pavel in order to meet his father, a general.*
>
> *Gogolnik does not seem to have the proper interest in class struggle and hatred. He is too easy going.*

Then he meets Sasha. Sasha Ashtimova.

Crusty, on a night off, takes his despoiled American dreams to the Palace of Trade Unions, which has been rented by some Yaroslavl institutes for a dance. Most of the music is American. The party is pretty boring, a biggish affair where Crusty knows hardly anyone and it all seems a little drab, without a future, until a girl in a Western hairdo, à la Jane Fonda, with a green dress and black slippers comes in late. With the shine already off the other girls, it is like bringing in a foreign flag. The dress is Chinese brocade. And Crusty shuffles up for a dance.

"In America," he says, pulling her closer, "we dance this way."

Sasha is a Moscow girl who has been thrown out of her home by her stepfather, and come to Yaroslavl to live with an aunt. She is studying at the Foreign Languages Institute. When her stepfather would lock her out of their Moscow apartment at night she would have to sleep on the landing. It interests her that Crusty is an American.

Sasha is looking for love, in love with love. In Moscow, however, a friend of hers even taught her to do it for money once. Now she has several boyfriends, at once, though she is careful. But there is something restless about Sasha, something wanton. It is as if sex, or love at least, is a way to get away from ideology. Besides, she has learned to get her supper free and yet pay no more than a kiss and a promise. Now suddenly she has an American in her collection.

Crusty's Russian, of course, is very basic, though he boasts to her that he knows how to say, "Turn off the light," and "Kiss me."

But she is studying English and the opportunities to talk in American are not so many. He does not like to talk about his country, though, and sometimes says strange things, like, "I have the soul of a beggar. Some day I will be a bum and free as a bird."

"We have no bums in Russia," says Sasha.

"Yes, but a man in Russia, and a girl too, they have their own souls. You are born with a soul. It is your possession. Your birthright. In America we have private property and the pursuit of happiness, but not soul."

This interests her. He explains that Americans are all born with a *tabula rasa*– a blank blackboard, an empty sheet– instead of a soul. There is no yesterday, no tomorrow. Consumption takes the place of desire. Success takes the place of feeling. Money takes the place of emotion.

"What about the American dream?" asks Sasha.

"The American dream is the opiate of the masses," says Crusty. "It is a television box full of pictures, with advertisements in between. The dream is an advertisement. It is a new tooth paste for a smile. A set of smiling white teeth. An aspirin. A product. There is a big package and nothing inside."

Sasha is impressed. She thinks of Pushkin, of Dostoevsky, of Tolstoy, Of Gogol. Of vodka, and good Russian bread.

"America," says Crusty, "is big bright red lips and no kiss. Even Marilyn Monroe committed suicide."

Sasha kisses him. It is a warm moment in the Cold War. He scarcely looks like Thomas Jefferson. But then he doesn't look like Stalin either. The names turn in mind: Chicago, New York, Hollywood, Texas. She has seen Gene Kelly in Anchors Away and Singin' in the Rain— maybe America is like that? Blue jeans and dancing and cars and house of her own!

Crusty would take her to a never-never land where there is no mud, no Kostya, no Yuri, no Anatoly, no Banner of Youth and Red State and Socialism to build and where they drink Scotch and soda, Gin and tonic, and Bloody Marys. At least Crusty isn't a dumb worker.

On the other hand, he is American. Maybe a spy. In 1938, it was enough just to be Polish to be put in political prison, in concentration camp. Her aunt reminds her of that. A foreigner is always a risk, but Sasha is more modern, less Soviet— her heart and hopes lead her head. Besides, she never suspects that Crusty will one day be a bum.

KGB file from June 10:
> *There is a general opinion that Gogolnik will never be a worker. He is slack. Careless. Inattentive. He has no enthusiasm for the political meetings compulsory lectures. He seems more interested in shopping, the girls, and his apartment.*

Dimitri reports that Gogolnik is always talking about the Russian soul. He has no interest in the Soviet System. He talks a lot about humanity, not production. He seems to think the soul is a real thing, like a tractor. So far, however, he has not tried to go to Church. He is fond of saying America is a "big package with nothing inside," although he may say this just to impress the authorities. He has taken up with a Moscow girl called Sasha Ashmitova, a girl of suspicious reputation. They met at a Palace of Trade Unions dance.

Sasha visits Crusty in his apartment by the river after their first kiss, a tentative affair in the snow under a bridge.

He lives in a grand building but his apartment is very small. Not even cozy. It is what they call *kasyono*, this is, bureaucratic–lacking in home atmosphere. "Iron dust," as they say. His table is *neobtyosoniy*– not polished properly. He has ordinary shop chairs and a bookcase put together of a few boards.

He has boasted to her that he has a lot of books in English, but when she gets there all he has is Marx and Engels and Lenin in translation.

"Marx writes like an engineer," he says, and she smiles.

The moon is on them like a skin, a sheaf of water. She thinks of him like an overcoat. An overcoat is the shape of his soul. In Gogol's story, the thieves took Akakie Akakeievich's new overcoat from him. It was in the Department of … but it is better not to name the Department. No respect was shown him in the Department. One day, however, he had an overcoat, and that was it.

He is not a soldier, however, nor is Crusty. Not even an official. Perhaps there is hope. The hands of the night are warm. He is an American. She naked in the arms of a spy. She helps him, and trembles with excitement. He is not rough. He is not Russian. The bed takes up most of the apartment. The bed and the moon.

Perhaps it is Crusty's bravest moment. There is no telling. We know so very little about him.

It is 1988, and the varnish is peeling. The grim, reactionary reality of the Brezhnev years is over, but the cynicism remains. Star Wars has finally bankrupted the Soviet Union, and communism is no longer the promise of the future, no longer the hope of economic fraternity. Crusty is even unemployed.

In fact he was fired some years ago from his job at the Yaroslavl Plastics Factory and has never found anything since. On the outskirts of town he still collects firewood and goes from house to house selling kindling, but what keeps him alive is the 700 rubles a month he still gets– 70 new rubles now– from the Russian Red Cross.

His bag is packed. It is an empty thing. Scarcely a shirt in it. No memories even. He cannot remember what life has done with him. It seems to be a garbage can where somehow he has ended up behind the house and the truck is coming to collect him.

Is it a farm? An apartment house? A wooden cottage? Shostakovich– was he not also censured by the State? Those bombastic symphonies. Had he not heard them? Maybe the KGB has finally cracked his case; they are taking him to the Kremlin for questioning. He has never been inside the Kremlin. The onion towers.

"Commissar," he says, when they call him in to make the announcement, "Don't you believe in the Russian soul?"

The Commissar makes a bitter sound of *glasnost*, like breaking glass, and answers, "Comrade, we no longer believe even in the System."

Crusty spends his last days wandering around the streets, as if he were looking for a lost child. Or maybe he is hunting for an American spy– himself. Or Sasha. Or wood for kindling. Then they detain him to get him off the streets until the plane leaves.

1917-1988: it is a long time. They give him some money and his old passport, long out of date, a sort of Rip van Winkle of the Cold War.

Sometimes he realizes in his sadder moments that maybe Sasha is behind it, maybe Sasha has no longer vouched for him– maybe Sasha has reported him to the authorities. She has been the accomplice of his deportation. Despite their romance; despite the years.

At the end, having a defector, a misfit, is too much for her and when the System collapses, his life collapses too. He depended on the Cold War for his identity. Now Sasha, now the Soviet Union has no more need of Crusty, no use for a pawn of ideology, and the century that chewed him up now is ready to spit him out. He is a useless tear in the eye of time.

Crusty thinks of himself as a snowman. A chronicler of winters. A black hat on and a Russian carrot in his mouth. Some child with his father made him out of snow and he froze to ice. There is no record of birth or begetting in him, no memory of Piraeus, even, when he said farewell to the West. The Soviets have wanted to know what his father was. This is still important in Communism. "I had no father," he said. He remembers that. It had not impressed the organs.

A holiday in Greece seemed to the organs a very unlikely trip for the son of nobody, a bastard. So be it. It was some kind of cruise, with her, perhaps a honeymoon trip– the soul: the Greek soul.

That had been Crusty's objective, the *anima* that inspired Democracy, the City State, the Olympics, the Parthenon. There was some sculpture of the God, of Apollo, in a magazine, and it seemed

102

like a beacon— something quite different than baseball, football, hockey, basketball. Yes, he had told her of it. Told the Commissar too.

The century is now a reverie, from the car, the early Ford, to the Empire State building, the movies, the airplane, the telephone, TV— the worker State. The Kremlin. It is all topsy-turvy. And now he is to lose Sasha, too, as a man loses a photograph, as a newspaper turns from the First World War to World War II, to Korea, Vietnam, and then is blown away with the dead, papers of burnt out days, wrappers to Eternity, and Crusty, with suitcase, is under detention in a building of the organs and has his plane ticket and is on the way back to the United States— land of opportunity.

A cup of coffee. He no longer recognizes even the photo of himself in the passport— his life is being returned to him: opportunity, the pursuit of happiness. And Sasha, his soul, is being taken away from him. But was she ever his? Beyond him. A different tongue. Aerflot will take him. *Perestroika.*

The State is no longer interested in Crusty. His fat file is no longer a part of production.

From the KGB file:

Gogolnik is not suitable material for the worker's Republic, and if this is a cover for clandestine contact and intelligence in the Soviet Union, it appears to be a very sophisticated but useless disguise since Gogolnik's knowledge and actions constitute no danger to State security.

He is, however, a threat to Soviet society in a larger sense, as a role model and American presence. Something is subversive about a man without attitude, as Gogolnik largely seems to be, without loyalties, beliefs, principles, ideology, and his constant harping on the soul of man is annoyance to all communists and the State. It is the opinion held by certain people that 70 new rubles a month still stipended for this residential non-citizen is too much and is a waste of State funds.

Gogolnik's coming to the Soviet Union has served no proletarian purpose that can be perceived, and since it now seems clear that he is not even a spy, he is of no use to counterintelligence. Gogolnik now spends his time scavenging kindling wood and etcetera....

In his room of departure, a cot and bare walls, Crusty is wanted by the Commissar for a last interview– a reckoning.

"You can be happy," the Commissar says, "that with the advent of free enterprise in Russia we are returning you to America. Of course, you owe the State all that we have given you, minus the wages at the Yaroslavl Plastic Works. The Red Cross money, the apartment. And the woman. We loaned you a Russian woman. How are you going to repay?"

Crusty blinks. "What about my pension?"

"You have social security," says the Commissar.

"My *Russian* pension," say Crusty.

"It will pay back the State advances to you."

"I want to take my soul with me," says Crusty.

The Commissar looks at him incredulously. Then he sneers: "The mouse is not larger than the cat, comrade." And there is nothing more to say.

Crusty's heart cries with a song. Volga, Volga... or no, is it, "I sing a song of myself..."

Sasha does not come to see him at the station; Sasha of the almond eyes. The great promise of the Socialist future is over... there is no tomorrow. Only America. The city. A deadbeat's street.

The millennium stares at Crusty like a one-way street, and all his unlived fears crowd on the shores of the New World. He is an immigrant to his own country, to his own old age...he does not even know the name of the President.

They give him a few dollars and put him on the plane.

A flight into homelessness. At immigration, the American guard routinely checks his old passport, looks him in the face, and waves him on. Odd face, that one. Already upon reentry, he has forgotten Russia. All but the soul.

Yes, Crusty is back, but America is nowhere to him. A place without address on an empty street.

part three

Crusty's first American nocturne back in the West, his first
encore, is not spent in the airport Hilton, with its deluxe empty extra
rooms, cozy complete bathrooms, warm lounge meals, and cocktail
bar. Most of the Hilton chain, five year plans notwithstanding, has
been built since Crusty's time. Capitalism has expanded. Conrad
Hilton, self-made man, is even dead. Not only the hotel, but
everything looks bigger if not better than Crusty remembers– the
trucks, busses, cars, the airport itself. Not that things were small in
Russia. Grandiose, maybe, is the word. Proletarian.

He has eaten and watered himself on the plane. Beef Stroganoff.
Tray style, à la Aerflot. He has even got a Russian salami in
his suitcase. He goes punctually and hygienically to the public
bathroom in the airport. At the customs shops it is Versace, Armani,
Billy Bass. Perfumes. Who are these people?

He honestly doesn't remember the great American latrine so
grand either. The busy airport seems to be a whole megalopolis,
and maybe he could just settle down here for the night in one of
the leatherette chairs. It would solve a lot of bother. The number of
uniformed guards around, however, dampens his plans.

America. Lots of blacks; no blacks in Russia. He almost
wonders if, after all, he will gain a new stake in life ... perhaps
he could even work here, right at the airport, start tomorrow, never

leave. Live here with the giant planes landing and taking off. Never have to go inland. Never arrive.

The anonymous bank automats puzzle him. They look like little 5 & 10¢ store snack bars, or dispensers, where the automated sandwiches and candies used to be behind glass, but he has no credit card– never has seen one.

Crusty is not a plastic man: Cirrus, 24-Express, Visa. These are new names to him on the horizon. The only card he can remember is Social Security, but he has long since lost it, forgotten his nine-digit number. Social Security should have automatic tellers.

There must be some left-over office in the bustling city that would expedite his Social Security, he thinks, but he cannot remember– and he isn't yet 65. In Russia he was Ashmitova, or Alyosha, as they called him in Yaroslavl.

The shores of America beckon to the poor, the maimed, the downtrodden– somewhere he remembers that. From the looks of Capitalism, however, there won't be much kindling to gather, not many traditional fires. The New World seems to be on automatic.

He is toting his soiled bag. It is the same one he had with him when he went to Russia, only now it has a few Soviet shirts, an extra pants, a salami, mittens, his first Russian hat, and mostly old Yaroslavl newspapers in it. He does not know why he packed the newspapers. Back in Yaroslavl he thought maybe they would be valuable in the United States; he could sell them; souvenirs; or prove he was there. Now all that is behind him.

He looks, in fact, like an immigrant, not a street person– his faded clothes are much worse than an American bum's. Much more citified. More worn out.

He is also scared to linger in the terminal, but the ferocious taxis mean nothing to him– there is no place to go. No address of arrival. No home. He guesses he is here, wherever it is. So he walks out the ramp, timidly, following the traffic and endless flow of destination and arrival, the life of clocks, people coming, people going, lugging his bag and duly comes to the classic Hilton Hotel, oval drive, entrance, marquee, doorman, lights. He momentarily stands transfixed looking at the entrances and exits, as if America were a revolving door.

110

Befuddled, knowing this is not for him, he then continues around the rectangular side of the huge building, past the laundry entrance, past the service entrance, past the parking lot, with its omnivorous looking machines, like a hyper-junkyard, a mechanized playground, and haltingly comes to the loading ramps in the back of the hotel, and a bulky dumpster. Trash and dust bins are stashed there in the dark. Ash cans have certainly changed, he thinks. An empty dumpster, The Hilton dumpster. A luxury dumpster.

Crusty gets in.

It is already raining. Lights gleam in the empty yard and Crusty peers out wondering whether a night's lodging is safe. It is already dark. He makes himself comfortable, takes out his salami, and has himself a bite. He props up the suitcase as a pillow, with a few of the old Yaroslevl newspapers, and leans back. He is tired.

The final flight from Moscow, from exile, is a long one, but it is the grievous years that weigh on him, the lack of memory in getting back to the land of the free, the home of the brave. All those miles. All those faces. All those years. All that propaganda. Inside his painted and rusted dumpster, after all, he has been a first hand witness to the fall of Communism, the end of the Red Menace, the collapse of the Evil Empire. He saw it with his own bleary eyes. He has the Cyrillic newspapers from Yaroslavl to prove it. And as if graced by God's blessing, with greetings from Uncle Sam, he has a dry dumpster to himself to ward off the free world rain and the cold.

As he goes to sleep, he remembers Gene Kelly dancing in Singin' in the Rain, in love with Debbie Reynolds, the rain coming down in buckets, the street full of puddles, the lamppost. That was long before he ever left. Was it Debbie or Sasha? Inside the frigid dumpster, it is all the same. But he dreams of music, an accordion playing Beautiful Heaven, filling the dumpster with song.

Love does not come in a can. This Crusty dreams in the dumpster. It is not a song, not a movie, not a dance– but an advertising slogan. A negative promotion. Somehow it sums up Crusty's wayward life, especially in his present accommodations.

There is no central heating in a dumpster, but Crusty does not awake. Instead, he sees a giant billboard in his dream that says,

"Love does not come in a can." The slogan advertises no product, there are no mounted cowboys smoking Marlboros– no picture even. No product. But the message seems somehow relevant to Crusty, somehow to fit his new living arrangement. He even dreams of staying on here, in the dumpster, making it his home– acquiring a car, mail delivered, furniture, and a TV. Dumpsterdom, USA.

Mendicant night is not all dreams. In the dumpster with Crusty is a trapped rat, hunkered down in the opposite corner. The rat is hungry, so Crusty throws him a chunk of salami. The poor and the outcast share their fate.

Mostly he sleeps, a jumbled movie of his return to the USA running by his numb dreams. In it Uncle Sam scolds him for going to Russia, but then turns beneficent, and says, "Sorry, son, we can build airports, roads, skyscrapers, bridges, sewers, and cities, open super markets with dazzling displays of food, take care of the world's poor and downtrodden, but unfortunately there is just no place for you. You rejected our goodwill– your license, your draft card, your social security number, your credit cards, and your long distance phone card, your registration, your life insurance, your welfare payments, your annuities, your liability insurance, your medical programs, your unemployment insurance, your bank account insurance and all the other benefits of our society, so now you will just have to brave it alone, son, at the shelter, the inn, the soup kitchen, wherever, but remember: you are where you are– it's the land of the free!"

Uncle Sam, in star-spangled red, white, and blue, is full of good will. Crusty just doesn't take to any of it. A man's character is his fate, and Crusty's homecoming is just that– if one could say he has a character, or a fate. In a way all Crusty wants is existence, and his expectations are low at that. He is more of pigeon than a man. Yet something is out of whack, because American cities teem with gray pigeons.

The last time Crusty has been in a Humpty-Dumpty is during the army. It comes back to him. He is out on a field maneuver: the exercise is Mines and Booby traps. Captain Mason is lecturing to the recruits on mines and booby traps. Crusty, in fatigues, is in the grandstand. Captain Mason has a bad stutter: "... this manual 330B

112

on mmmmmmmmmines and bbbbbbbbbooby traps," the Captain reads, and then Crusty spots another officer surreptitiously crawling under the grandstand about to detonate firecrackers.

Crusty stands up, raises his hand, and blurts out, "CCCCCCCaptain Mmmmmmmmason, I'd like to report that Mmmmmmmmmmajor Nnnnnnnivens is under the grandstand about to set of a bbbbbbbbbooby tttttttttrap…."

The company punishment is to shovel out the Dumpster, hose it down on the inside, then arduously shovel all the garbage back in to the Humpty-Dumpty. But then, in basic training, Crusty has no dreams. He doesn't even know that in his own future he will come to rely on Dumpsters for food and lodging.

Now he dreams. He dreams that all life is a comic book. A story board with a series of stills of him, Crusty, panning for bread, a kind of Bugs Bunny gone wrong, people saying ludicrous things in balloons, like, "The bum thinks he's a millionaire," and, "He lives on the beach, next door to his friend," and, "Why does he beg with two hands? Because business is so good that he opened a branch office."

The more he dreams the more of a riddle is his life. "I am from somewhere," he dreams,

"America is my heritage, and if I want to decipher the tangle of contradictions and illusions around me, I am first going to have to learn to decipher America."

If he is going to live out the fate of a bum in America, he is going to need to know what that means. That means the streets. It does not occur to him to decipher himself.

His social security card haunts him too. He imagines it as a billboard just outside the airport terminal welcoming him back to America. The number is lit up in black ciphers. But he cannot read it. It is a blur. The card itself spills out of heaven with other dancing cards, the credit card, the bank card, the phone card, the insurance card, and like jokers and aces, and kings and queens and jacks of diamonds they dance down the street as he enters America from the airport, a choreography of plastic cards posting the way with bright music from the airport ramps to the tunnel byways and markers of the life Crusty has returned to.

113

For most people America is the world of the movies. The movies and TV is all they have left of oblivion. But for Crusty oblivion and the real world merge into one; the theater, where the lone bum is in from the rain and eating popcorn while the screen spins out the celluloid illusion of credit cards, comedy, romance, adventure, is the same as real life, the real footage of the bum, Crusty, walking with his bag down the tarmac, out the terminal onto the ramps and taking up his abode in the Hilton dumpster.

He may not be the hero of his own life, but he is the start of his own film– his solitary tramping silhouette projected against the background of the ramps, the traffic, the skyline. Whereas most people pay a ticket of admission to see some show of their own life, some escape, Crusty is acting out his own story– meeting the imaginary marks on the eerie set of Soul Street. Because he is outside normal life, he is inside his own movie.

His world, in fact, is a cruel cinema realité where the marginal tramp is on stage. The prop is a garbage can. The clothes. The food. The walk. The dumpster. He doesn't have to pay admission to his own life, however. The celluloid of his own situation is already like a scenario captured on film. Crusty, in his dumpster, is like a Hollywood take, a poster promotion– he looks like a movie poster. No costume is needed. The new life around him is as stark as any realist set. It is not a documentary, but a feature starring the homeless Crusty as himself.

In his steely lodging, he dozes quietly into the dawn unaware of the big trucks and the coming early shift. No punch clock calls him, no simmering coffee, no newspaper slipped under the door. The things of this world do not have their grasp on Crusty. He is an outsider even to the workaday world.

But the System comes to get him. At 6 A.M., the big blue BFI truck rolls up behind the Hilton, backs up to Crusty's dumpster, forks the bin, and lifts his container, Crusty and all, onto the asshole of the garbage truck and tips it into the bin. Crusty, with the frantic rat, loses his precarious perch, his home for the night, and tumbles out of bed into the BFI bin. A rag of human rubbish.

The fork lift returns to the bin, and there in the well of the garbage truck, floundering with his suitcase, is the exile returned,

Crusty the tramp, initiated into his new life, and the garbage man gives a laugh.

"Where are your rubbers?" he bellows, about to throw the lever, the rotator that would sweep Crusty into the belly of the truck and compress him like an old milk container.

"Rubbers?" says Crusty, dazed, dirtied, bruised.

"Well, if you want to work with us, you'll need your rubbers."

Good morning, America, is a more than a rude awakening.

The raucous gang at the shelter says it will be a potato roast, out under the bridge, but it turns out to be a pigeon roast.

They have caught the piteous birds in the park, pretending to feed them some stale bread. They threw a tarpaulin over them and stuffed them in a burlap bag. There are about twenty. Pigeons. What could be more commonplace? When Crusty gets there they are plucking their feathers.

"Squab," Meathead grins, with his teeth like a minefield.

Crusty has come out with Barney, a flat-faced bum who has shown him the ropes at the shelter. Barney is harmless. Overhead, high above the pylons, traffic rocks on the sweeping bridge and the noise of heavy treads falls to earth here in no-man's land, just some scuffed earth and litter and the slack river underneath. The fire is going. It smokes.

There is beer. Someone has taken apart an old rusty grille and made spits for the pigeons. In the coals there are also potatoes wrapped in tinfoil. Someone has brought french fries, potato chips, and pickles.

The looming industrial city seems like a postcard around them, the vagrant men in their jackets and boots, nobody to bother them. The grade from the pylons slopes down slowly to the grimy river. Smoke stacks by the water spout steam. Lots and yards full of containers score the landscape. And overhead the far-off traffic of civilization rumbles, on its way to and from the far-off houses, the malls, the offices, the homes. Instead, these men eye the roasting pigeons.

"Just like barbecuing Vietcong," Meathead says as he skewers a pigeon.

Barney is turning the potatoes. The hoboes bunch around the fire warming their hands and leggings. It doesn't even look like a road gang– no helmets, no orange jackets. Not a pack of scavenger birds either, vultures. The homeless are too stocky and stolid, in their jeans, boots, and Alaskan parkas to look like birds. Not gaunt enough for wolves either. But there is something of the call of the wild in them, something of the pack.

Their turf is the no-man's land of progress, the terrain under the public suspension bridge, where no cars can reach, no access is provided. Wasteland, empty lots, medians, industrial yards. A campfire, pigeons, and a straggle of vagrants. It is not the Fourth of July.

"We should have Worcestershire sauce," someone says.

None of the bag ladies have been invited either. It is a stag party. Men on the loose, but then, just as the birds are browning up, Madeleine and fat Rosie approach. Someone told them about it, and in her cart Madeleine is toting several gallons of cheap wine.

"Fucking ladies," says Meathead, as they approach. Even so, it isn't exactly high society.

"Next thing you know," adds Meathead, "we'll have a fuckin' weddin' on our hands. Hey, Crusty, you wanna dance?" But there is no music. Not even a portable radio. Barney had one, stolen, but he sold it.

These are men without music. Men without melody. Even the accordion would toot a tune alien to these men's existence. It might do for Crusty, a jig, or a Polanaise, a sort of Parisian slum round, or cabaret, or circus music. That's what it needs. Circus music. The sad clown.

Crusty would respond. And Federico Fellini's camera, on the outskirts of the city. The building lots, the mud, the cranes, the dump trucks. Crusty, eyeing Madeleine, would not mind a tune. Get

118

him off the breadline, out of the soup kitchen. But the ground is silent. The men huddled around as if in the pockets of a depression. Off the girders of the rusted bridge seagulls soar.

The human gaggle, even with the fire, has something lugubrious about it, something desolate and volcanic, as if these men were bunched around a tomb or a fire hole in the ground to hell. A sulphur vent.

The trouble is they are not in a painting. It is not a canvas. As a painting, this would be a classic scene, hobo culture, vagrants, vagabonds— a picaresque picnic on the outskirts of modern industrial culture with these men warming their hands at the hearth of life. But it is not a painting. Canvas has not romanticized the huddle. They are standing in the verisimilitude of reality, in the mud.

The pigeons at least have paid the piper. These are not Cornish hen from the super market. These are the doves of the Commons. The pedestrians of the bird world, no more strutting, pecking for crumbs; now they are on the spit.

Meathead crassly wants to put ketchup on them. Madeleine has an extra bottle in her cart. The blood of the tomato. He barbecues the birds in it, like sauce. It reminds Meathead of the carnage in Vietnam, and he tries to put some on Crusty, to paint him up a little.

"Never had a bullet through your eye," Meathead says, squirting ketchup in Crusty's face. Macabre maquillage. Crusty looks like blood is dripping from the grimace of his face and Meathead hoops. It is Heinz's. Theresa, the Heinz heiress, is worth 578 million dollars— more with the market rising— and these men, between them, even with Madeleine and Rosie's pockets, can't ante up $50.

Crusty's heavy heart is like one of the roasting pigeons, a spit through it. Not like a soaring gull. Yet, to the right, the bridge; to the left, the river; behind him a pylon; in front of him, the fire. There is no greater happiness. Being a bum is the true Zen, the art of nothingness— but Crusty is not even conscious of annihilating all that's made to a dim thought in a dim shade.

The shadow of the bridge. All that is progress roaring above them metal girders like gulls, cantilevered, suspended— but theirs is the shade of the engineer's marvelous, the brave mockery of technology. They have no place in the sun, but under the ramparts. There are no rockets in air, no loud glare. Sticks and stones. A few sentences carved in drudgery out of bone and gristle.

Madeleine sings a few bars of a popular song in a coarse, rough voice, and grabs Rosie. For a moment, while the fire sizzles, they dance in front of the grilling pigeons. It is as if they had brought their sewing. Even destitution knows a party. But Meathead and the men look sullenly on; only Crusty smiles.

He turns his pockets out, cocks his Russian cap, and does a jig. Meathead is disgusted and throws a beer can at him. He picks up the empties and his cronies join in, pelting Crusty as he continues his jig. Only Madeleine fights back, returning the fire of beer cans.

"Goddamn dancing," Meathead cries. "You'd think we was a ballroom. Tough guys don't dance." He has heard it somewhere.

Norman Mailer's worst line, afloat in desolation, sounds different than in the effete parlors of New York, but it appeals to Meathead. To Crusty, instead, the moment is always from here to eternity— that's how he lives. But Crusty and Meathead are living literature, living the literal, not writing it. Their book is the crawl from dawn to dusk, and dusk to dawn. And God, not Norman Mailer, has written the bleak script.

Under the bridge has the dank yet at the same time dry odor of stale air that unbegotten places do, where it never dries, where it never gets wet. The rain doesn't wash here, yet the sun never shines. The sear grass never grows, the thrown away papers and plastic bags are the only artificial flowers. It is here that the hoboes might bury their dead; it is here they party in a kind of necropolis.

Sounds of sirens from the city, an ambulance on the bridge, wail on the fringes of this gloom like a toneless soundtrack of the city, the city bleating its pain and its emergency— the sound of accidents, and stopped hearts, and frantic frustration. Everybody above has to get somewhere, but here below the men have nowhere to go.

Not even TV has much meaning for a bum. A litany of empty pictures that promote toothpaste for the toothless, cars for the wheelless, food for the hungry, pills for the numb, vacations for the homeless. NBC, CBS, ABC should bring their cameras under the bridge sometime and advertise no-man's land. The garden of garbage.

The debris is a kind of flea market of refuse, a helter-skelter dump, a stretch of environmental warfare. It is as if chance discarded a few old pots, a gutted ice box, boards and tar paper— and this gaggle of bums; survivors of America's revolving door. Beggars in the land of surplus butter.

"The birds are done," Barney calls, and the motley company, like craven cats in an empty lot, gather round and whet their whiskers.

"Those are pigeons," says Crusty, "That's not squab."

"Listen to him," Meathead howls.

"Have a potato," Madeleine says.

"I don't eat pigeon," Crusty announces.

Meathead rears up. "Now, dainty, ain't we. Our little Russian sputnik don't eat pigeon. Christ be damned. But that's a shame. You oughtta tell it to the mayor. Goddamn commie. So we're a vegetarian, are we?"

"Nope," says Crusty, "But pigeons have souls. I don't eat souls."

"Oh, a soul, is it?" hollers Meathead. "So pigeons have souls, do they? Well, we have bellies, man. You cockeyed piece of shit, there is no soul where we come from, and I have half a mind to ram a pigeon down your throat and a skewer up your ass. You're lucky you're not on the spit yourself, you little turd-assed mother fucker."

Meathead picks up one of the spits and makes a lunge at Crusty. Then he is coming at him with the spit full throttle, and Crusty backs off.

"Fuckin little preacher," Meathead cries, throwing the spit like a spear at him.

But Madeleine, the bag lady, comes up to Meathead and starts pummeling him with her fists and kicking his shins, so Crusty gets away.

"Another pigeon," Meathead hollers, bowls Madeleine over, and retreats to the fire. "Get that bum outta here or I'll piss in his puddle."

121

"And you," Madeleine cries from the ground where she has fallen, "You've got the face of a pig farting."

Crusty helps her flounder to her feet.

"Get outta here or I'll kill the both of you," Meathead grunts, hard by the other bums around the fire. Together, Crusty and Madeleine push her cart. The pigeon roast is over.

Overhead the endless traffic rolls, and the bridge sways on its suspenders.

Vagabonds, in the East, are often the hidden Holy man—untouchables, but possibly God in disguise. The post-modern bum, instead, is no longer politically correct. That is Crusty's case— even before he starts talking absent-mindedly to pigeons.

A bum is an inmate of his own mind. Often he is ambulatory. A psychotic pigeon. Crusty does not even know the words for what he is. Whatever he is. Except the time the Harvard research team took him in for testing. They came to the shelter and took six of them— $25 apiece. Psychologists. In suits.

After testing him on the reflex thimble, a little button he is supposed to punch as many times in a minute as he can, with his index finger, they ask him if he hears voices.

"I hear the pigeons. I hear you," Crusty says.

"No," says the psychologist. "I mean real voices. Voices that aren't there."

This stumps Crusty. "All the voices that I hear are there," he says. "How can I hear a real voice if it isn't there?"

That stumps the psychologist. "What do the pigeons say?" he asks.

"Oh, lots of things. Nothing you'd be interested in."

In fact, he goes to St. Leonard's Peace Garden in the North End, the first Church edifice built in New England by Italian immigrants, where the primroses grow, where the mums deck the brickworks, where he can sit on the wall and talk to pigeons.

The curate comes out once and says, "Son, these pigeons can only talk Italian." But he doesn't throw him out.

In his mind, Crusty is not a psychotic– he is a pigeon. Even the pigeons seem to think so, although what Crusty likes about these birds is that they don't think, they don't know words– they just get out of the way.

A pigeon is forever in motion, not high-minded; its neck bobs back and forth to the accompaniment of its feet, as if it couldn't think. Pigeons look everywhere but seem to see nothing. They are not organized enough even to store their own food.

Bread flies off from their beaks as they shake a bite loose and flies loose somewhere where they can't even find it. They have no thumbs. They lose sight of the bread, even standing right on top of it.

Besides, the one thing a pigeon is truly wary of is being stepped on. Like Crusty.

Crusty himself has a habit of movement like pigeon, that is, when a lady comes down the street Crusty scuttles into the gutter until the lady passes. He just stands there, in the curb. If she is pretty, he doffs his hat. He used to. But they took it as an insult. So he gave up the hat part and just stands aside in the gutter.

The iridescent pigeons too are scared of the boot. The foot, the boot is their level. Pigeons have no manners but they will do almost anything to get out of the way. In fact, this is what pigeons and the homeless spend their days doing. Cars. People. Other animals. But pigeons don't listen. They are immune to everything but bread and the boot.

Crusty's talks with the pigeons are almost one-way conversations.

"Psssh," says Crusty. The birds cock their walks the other way, ready to fly– but they always have the bum in one eye. They can only see sidewise. Little orange eyes. But, unless there is food, it is as if they hear nothing.

So Crusty collects the bits of bread old ladies and other donors leave for the pigeons, then he feeds the birds their own food. The dole.

"I am a bum based on real life," he tells the birds. No answer.

The birds want the food, not the talk. In the animal kingdom, food is real, talk is shallow.

"The lot of man is quiet desperation," he tells them. He remembers that one, like a stray straw, from school somehow. Or did his father used to say that?

Sometimes he reads them the newspaper from the trash can. Items about what is happening in Washington. The periscopes.

The pigeons show no sign of understanding. Pigeons don't understand newspapers. They're interested in survival, not death and disaster. Yet they don't seem deaf, either. Just obtuse. They respond with noises– they cluck and they coo. They hear each other. But the human voice has no effect on them, as on a dog. Even a cat. Pigeons are dumb to words. Like bums. "Do you know what I had for lunch?" Crusty asks them. Silence. Like talking to the wind.

So he says to them, "You can leave a wife, but you can't leave an ex-wife."

Maybe he is thinking of Sasha. A woman, once you have left her, is always with you. Even if it is she who has left.

Pigeons apparently do not have wives because this makes no impression on them either.

He wonders if there are insane pigeons, dysfunctional pigeons. It wouldn't be Darwinistic. The fittest survive. Yet insanity continues. What function, what selection, does insanity serve? Why does nature select the insane gene for preservation? Crusty seems to remember something of this from his Leninist books. There is no rhyme or reason to what Crusty remembers. No clue. Nature in tooth and claw. Is that what pigeons are? Or bums– are they anti-Darwinistic?

So he tells them, "The difference between blessed madness and insanity is: insanity is following the wrong God."

Crusty does not know what that means, but Barney, at the shelter, showed it to him on a piece of paper. And he remembers it like the ear remembers a phrase of music from the radio. The

125

culture is blowing around. It sounds like something that would make sense to pigeons.

He looks up at the Church, A bulwark. The pigeons take no notice, like fellow bums, here a lame one, there a white one, as if they all had some endless business to attend to, impervious to distraction. Impervious to religion.

The difference between Crusty and St. Francis is not that they both talk to birds, but that when St. Francis talked, the birds listened. The difference between a saint and a bum. The audience.

"What's madness," Crusty says, "but nobility of soul at odds with circumstance." From Barney again. Barney is full of quotes. But the impervious pigeons, pudgy and feathered, remain oblivious.

Yet the pigeons inspire Crusty. He says to them, "To be, or not to be...," but he cannot remember the rest of that one. He wonders why the bums at the shelter are not as carefree a lot as the birds—no depression here, no gloom, no dirt, sweat, and grime. If he were a pigeon, Crusty thinks, he could at least belong. Maybe he would even have a friend.

Instead, at the shelter, it just gets worse. But Crusty is glad. More pregnant women are coming. More young people just out of high school, graduating onto the streets. Of course, they get more prison inmates too, from the halfway houses that are closing, and the detoxes show up too now that the centers are closing. But to Crusty the mix is better than skid row veterans alone. It alleviates the joint. Society. Not just your hard-core. Everybody is in it now. It increases the competition, but it improves the service. The ambiance.

So he says to the pigeons: "The main thing is being on your own recognizance." And he doesn't know it, but he has just defined liberty.

"Amen," the pigeons all say, looking at him.

Could he tell the Harvard psychologist, Dr. Freed, that the pigeons, like a choir, all said, "Amen" outside the Church of St. Leonard, in Peace Garden?

Not on your life. One of the rules of a bum is that you don't even know what you know. It is the right of ignorance.

So he tells that psychologist, "The difference between the pigeons and us is that they have a soul."

126

"A soul?" the startled Dr. Freed blinks. After all, he can't not believe in it. The soul is his business. His bread and butter. His crumb. But never have two men meant such different things by one word, Soul, as the psychologist and Crusty.

"Do you have a soul?" Dr. Freed asks, in his white coat.

Crusty peers back at him, impervious as a pigeon. "Amen," he says.

The psychologist leans forward, really interested now: "Tell me, what is the soul?"

Crusty looks at the ceiling. How much can a man want for twenty-five dollars?

"I refuse to answer on the grounds that I might incriminate myself."

The psychologist coughs.

Then on second thought, Crusty says, "How much is it worth to you?"

The psychologist coughs again.

Amen. The choir of pigeons has spoken. Liberty is the watchword. The animal kingdom, in its instinct, is wise beyond the reaches of man, but it has taken Crusty a long time to elicit a response. Birds are not interested in personal matters; discomfort, even hunger, means nothing to them. Only a principle of great import, like Liberty, draws from them a response, and Crusty, though he now believes he is hearing things, knows what draws a bird and a bum together. It is the open skies. Flight is another name for being on your own recognizance.

The curate passes by again. "I take it the birds are faithful in their responses?" he mutters, walking past.

And again the birds say, "Amen." But only Crusty hears them. He crosses himself after the curate passes, making sure the priest doesn't see. It might cost something.

A bum is a mirror sitting on a bench. The world goes by and is reflected. People see themselves. The pigeons teem in the eye of God, and feed like chastened thoughts upon the crumbs of life. Crusty is about to say something, pose some conundrum for the birds, when Madeleine, real as life, wheeling her cart, wrapped in her bathrobe, comes around the corner and joins him on the bench.

127

They say nothing. One of the roots of their relation is that they scarcely ever say anything to each other. They think together, instead. Silence is the sort of marriage between them, the unbroken peace they share.

He never asks her anything. Doesn't even greet her. She nestles her small hulk next to him the nearest thing to snuggling up, opens one of her bags and hands him some crusts. He takes them, breaks bread, and tosses the pigeons more food.

She has never even told him her story. Besides, her story has ended. She is a book that is finished, but hangs around, a lady to whom you bring old buttons to sew on. But her fingers are gnarled with arthritis and she would have trouble holding a needle. Even so, she slips a hand through Crusty's and the two of them sit there clinging for life.

She dreams of being married here, by the curate, beside the marble statue of Mary and her lambs. Then she would be Mrs. Crusty. She hands him more bread. Her thoughts are askew this morning, and she forgets what it was she wanted to tell him. Not tell him, but communicate– sit there thinking on the bench until he got the message.

Perhaps he is right. Marriage would only spoil a good relationship. But she has her dreams too. A welfare room for two. With a little burner, an ice box, and a radio. She remembers her mother listening to old time radio many sounds and sights ago. That's all she wants, to give Crusty a little dignity.

"Dignity is a decent meal," Crusty preaches to the birds, throwing them more bread. He says it to the pigeons, not to her.

But she says, "Amen," and pulls the lunch things out of her cart. No wine or beer here; this is a Church garden. She looks at him. No. She is determined. Forever seems a day. Yet she will not live forever on Soul Street, not spend eternity on Misery Corner.

He has gone into a funk. Tedium is the bane of homelessness—
the view from the curb mostly trash, hub caps, fenders, traffic, dust.
The ethic of the street is a kind of numb stoicism, a snail without
a shell, a turtle without a back. Memory fades like a forgotten
wrapper, the vagabond stripped of talismans, identity tossed like
a torn package into the trashbin. Today doesn't intersect with
yesterday, or tomorrow— time: all the same, a hobo eternity that is
safe only from the vicissitudes of bourgeois life.

So, seeing Madeleine, he decides to go on a spree— to
MacDonald's, and take her; Crusty is not one to bow to tedium.

"What will I wear?" Madeleine asks. "I can't go to the Ritz like
this."

"Make it Burger King," says Crusty. "A real upscale night.

"Really?" Madeleine says to him. "The whopper, and all?"

"Yup."

It isn't often the homeless eat out. Actually, for Crusty and
Madeleine, going to Burger King is like eating in. The fast food is
elegant dining. They even have doilies.

"It's not my birthday," Madeleine objects.

"It's Valentines," says Crusty, something like a blush ruddying
his crusty skin.

So down in the public park the two of them polish up their act and work up an appetite. It's not every place in the world, not like America, that offers bums someplace egalitarian to go, a safe harbor to eat. At populist prices. The automats that surfaced after the Depression used to do that, and bums hung out at the old drug store counters that served sandwiches and coffee.

But with the advent of Burger King, MacDonald's, KFC, and Taco Bell, even the homeless can have a night out in clean, contemporary surroundings, with access to the latrine, along with the rest of America. Only for Crusty and Madeleine this is not fast food– this is fine dining. A banquet.

They even get to wash their hands here before eating. And a booth for themselves. They get to see what the rest of the country, particularly the young people, look like. The food is, to them, like home cooking. The menu is à la carte. It beats even the deli and salad bar at the supermarket, and is cheaper. Besides, the food isn't seconds, like from the dumpster. You get your own portion, daintily wrapped, not just an anonymous bowl from the soup kitchen.

"Old MacDonald had a farm," Crusty begins to sing as they set off, "And on this farm there some pigs. Eeeyiieeeyio."

His husky voice warms up the street and Madeleine puts her arm through his. If a photographer wanted to advertise hamburgers, this would be his shot. Crusty and Madeleine, the bum and the bag lady, heading in to the house of the double arches for the ninetieth billion burger. Somewhere a cow died for this, and Crusty and Madeleine, though they have never been on a farm, somehow sense what it is worth.

As they swing through the doors, Crusty whispers to her, "Give us our daily bread...."

They stop to admire the red heart pinned up in the doorway, never imagining that St. Valentine was an early martyr who gave his blood for Christianity. In MacDonald's, St. Valentine might be a contemporary of Mickey Mouse. But the two of them linger at the hanging paper heart. It is only cardboard, but crisp, red, and shiny.

"What are you having?" Crusty asks her.

As if she didn't know. "If I had my way, she says, squeezing his arm. "I'd eat your heart out. Heartburger. I'd have heartburger."

They look avidly into the reflection in the glass doors to see that they are looking their best. The villa of the hamburger, all brick and glass, neat and modest. Outside the door neat evergreen shrubs dot the mulch. It's not hamburger heaven, the old joints before the time of industrial franchise, but it's America's, the 20th century's answer to a hot meal, and the brick hut that houses MacDonald's is the nearest thing to a villa Crusty and Madeleine will ever enter.

The scruffy line at the order counter is broken into three, and Crusty and Madeleine step between the polished brass rails and take their turn. Waiting is part of the festivity. On the counter are cardboard cut out crowns, painted and tinted, for the children, but Crusty takes two and hands one to Madeleine. They fold them together and put them on each other, King for a day, Queen for tomorrow.

"The tyrants of Burgerdom," Crusty says; Madeleine appreciates the lame humor. She appreciates anything.

It is their Big Event. Humor on Soul Street, jokes at Misery Corner, are lame like cripples, limping like bums. Thought, too, is running out. It's not that Crusty and Madeleine mean to be like old married couples, bonds worn out, nothing to say, it's just that on Soul Street the thoughts run thin. The homeless brain tires of consciousness, because Soul Street is an exercise in obliteration— or in avoiding obliteration.

Crusty somehow knows there is more. He would like to silence existence to get beyond it to a kind of nirvana, instead of all the urban hustle and bustle. He would like to tell this to Madeleine over the burger supper— but he lacks the words. Fortunately, she knows it all; she can, accompany his thoughts.

"A candle, please," Crusty says to the Spanish teenager who is traying their whoppers, fries, and combo. "A candle for the whopper combo."

They happen to have birthday candles on supply. The Spanish girl gives Crusty two, and he says, "We'll be back for the cake."

They shuffle to the handy sideboard and load up with mayonnaise, ketchup, mustard, and relish— each taking about twenty packs. Sugar, and salt and pepper, are free too. They set it all on the tray and it makes the dinner look festive, like supply

131

side. Economy originally meant householding and when they get to their seats by the window they stuff the extra condiments into their bulging pockets. Prepare! Prepare!

Anatomy of the whopper: sesame seeds sharpen taste and plump, juicy tomatoes wet the palate. Tangy onions make it more cultured, while the serrated edges make fresh pickles more appetizing and anchor the other condiments during that first crucial bite. Mayo and ketchup blend to create the perfect dressing– the happiest marriage of all condiments, while the stripes on flame-broiled patties of meat signify bona fide flavor. Lettuce, the leafy green, tops the whopper while the overall size and weight says Crusty and Madeleine are getting what they paid for– mouth watering euphoria. Get your burger's worth!

Coca Cola, the mighty soft drink, is the champagne of America; it accompanies their meal, two super larges, floating with ice, sparkling with bubbles. Ice is almost free in America. "But you can't eat ice," says Crusty, and Madeleine knows what he means.

"In the old days these places had dancing," she suggests.

Crusty picks up the fork and spoon, pairs them off, and hums: "Hey, diddle-diddle, the cat and the fiddle...and the fork jumped over the moon!"

In front of him, over his tray, he makes the fork dance with the spoon, a little jig in Crusty's two hands, a two-step of the silver. Only it is all plastic. White plastic in its wedding best. And a tear comes to Mother Madeleine's eye.

"The best is yet to come!" Crusty cries bravely, toasting her in Coca Cola.

"Don't we have it good," Madeleine says, no irony intended; irony is for the upper classes, about the discrepancy between reality and the ideal, a luxury attitude. But Madeleine doesn't have that. There is no discrepancy. For her a stick is a stick and stone is a stone. Existence has no room for attitude.

The cheap Valentine doilies under the meal are brightly printed with hearts, a labyrinth, and games. Enter the Valentine labyrinth, it says, and see if you can find your way out. "Hi, there," a heart smiles, with eyelashes and a mouth and eyes. "I'm your Valentine." "Woof, woof!" a dog barks in the corner of the mat, "be my woofy."

132

Crusty and Madeleine look like old children at these games. This is their level of decoration, like paper cups. Popping the straws out of their bags, they blow the paper at each other, as if it were a favor.

They unwrap their warm burgers; Crusty sticks the two candles in the buns, and lights them. They face each other staring at the little candles burning. Like themselves. Two tiny candles burning on the street. The world is a great wind. Two wax wicks in the whoppers. Two souls.

"The best is yet to come!" repeats Crusty. At least, because they don't have a living room, they aren't watching TV, like the rest of America. Because they have no home they need no escape. They don't have to peer into the magic box of illusion. Reality is their box.

Suddenly, somebody in the kitchen yells: "Fire! Fire!"

For a frightened moment Crusty and Madeleine think it is their candles. Guiltily, they blow them out. But from the kitchen comes the cry again, "Fire!" Suddenly there is smoke billowing out of the order counter into the room.

A voice yells, "Everybody out!"

They can hear a fire engine. It all goes so fast. The loud alarm wails up the street. Their villa is burning down. The 90th billion hamburger has been too much. Valentines is over. The Establishment is burning down. Supper isn't even done.

Crusty and Madeleine stuff their whoppers into their extra large pockets with the french fries and onion rings, still sipping their cokes. The place is filled with smoke and a fireman is entering the front door with a hose. Madeleine grabs her Valentine doily, and with Crusty heads for the exit.

There is no exit from beggardom, though, and Crusty and his bag lady are exposed on the street again, standing on the naked curb, munching the rest of their whoppers and watching the action. Crusty is thinking it is better not to have a home– what if America burns down, and there is no insurance? While Madeleine is forlornly thinking of her wedding plans all gone up in smoke.

She takes Crusty's arm, as smoke pours out of Burger King, and he murmurs, "The best is yet to come!"

"Amen," says Madeleine.

A love story is not always about those who lose their heart, but about those who find the heart's sullen inhabitants.

When the weather turns a little balmier, because a homeless life hangs a lot on the weather– rain or shine is not a matter of mood, but of survival– he takes to hanging out by the equestrian statue of George Washington on the Commons at the foot of Commonwealth Avenue. George, high, handsome, and mighty on his horse, is the one thing that sometimes brings tears to Crusty's eyes, The Declaration of Independence, Washington at the helm– it is too much for him, like a dauntless dream he would like to believe in.

The Swedish actress comes by.

At first Crusty doesn't recognize her– just a pretty lady, and he steps down in the curb, as is his habit, to let her pass. But Gypsy the dog recognizes him and wags over to smell his boots.

"Oh, it's you!" the actress cries, and next thing Crusty knows they are sitting on the bench talking.

"You see, I'm Swedish," she says, "In Sweden we have social welfare for all. There is no misery. Everybody is bought and paid for. You would be a king in Sweden."

"I'm a bum here," Crusty says, to reassure her.

"Yes, but not really. You are king of your own soul. You have a salvific effect on society, because you are one of Jesus' poor. The meek inherit the hearth and follow the Lord. You teach meekness."

Crusty beams. "Salvific?"

"Yes, she says, and reaches into her purse, giving him fifty dollars. "A psychiatrist, a doctor, a lawyer get $50 an hour, and more. Why shouldn't you?"

"Because I have nothing to say," Crusty answers.

"I can do the talking," the actress replies, "That is what the fifty dollars are for. It's called therapy. The rich talking to the poor."

"I see," says Crusty, sitting there like Sigmund Freud.

"Yes," says the actress. "You see, because intensity strives for novelty, mystery, and a certain elusiveness, some schizophrenics appear endlessly interesting."

"Schizophrenic? Salvific?"

"It doesn't matter," the actress responds. "Paradoxically it is their madness that mimics mystery and depth, and this quality sometimes inspires long-lasting fascination if not always love."

The dog looks up at this one, and Crusty thinks of his bag lady, Madeleine. He certainly hopes she won't walk by just now with the baloney.

"Love is a creative synthesis," the actress says.

Crusty nods.

She goes on. "Since the human soul is a psychological achievement, a response to and differentiation from the world, the fundamental issue is whether one has made one's soul one's own."

"Oh, yes," Crusty says, "But I have no social security until I'm sixty-five."

"I know you have. That's why I'm talking to you." She pets Gypsy, who looks up at Crusty. But he doesn't say anything more. He just coughs slightly under his breath. A regular professional.

"You see," she says, "Life is a seamless, dying whodunit. No real life can be solved. It is a mystery, a plot, and a body– and finding the murderer. The murderer is yourself. Love is even more complex. The only real solution is death, that unravels all stories. Death undoes the end. That is why I am an actress."

At this she bursts into tears. The dog starts panting and looks concerned. She takes out a handkerchief and starts drying her eyes. "Don't worry," she says, "I'll be alright. Just a moment to catch my breath." And she gets out her powder and lipstick and mirror and makes herself right again.

136

"A smile is the actress' mark," she goes on. "We are constantly being someone who we aren't. Having emotions that are not ours. Making a fiction of appearance, a fib of reality. But you are not. You are truth itself. You emote our real selves to us. You are the unrecognized hero of the city. The city is our story."

She is silent for a moment. Crusty looks solemnly straight ahead, still holding the fifty dollar bill.

"Ah," she sighs, "The still, sad music of humanity."

There is another pause. Crusty sneaks a look at her and thinks she is very beautiful. The dog wags its tail.

"A man's self-judgment," she says, "is all there is of conscience."

She takes another beat, then utters: "Most men lead lives of quiet desperation."

She is silent. Crusty thinks he should say something, so he says, "Down at the shelter, Barney, another bum, sleeps with a Barbie doll."

She looks around at the manicured park. The Department of Public Works has not yet planted the flowers, and she thinks of all those who dally with life. Herself, she is overlaid with a thousand obligations. Her life is a harried heart, her love a tattered token, her face a careful mark. She lives around the corner from the Ritz, and walks Gypsy in the Commons. Walking Gypsy is her happy hour.

But she is also an artist. The hassle of real life, in all its crude, articulate hardiness startles and saps her. She loves her dog. She loves her husband. She loves her career. But the monstrous, curdled insensibility of America life, like a truck out of control, erodes her sense of sensibility, her capacity for justice. Gypsy is her only child.

She looks around and an indescribable longing for the birches of Sweden fills her, the sweet village of her cities, the pristine roads, the cottages, the pastries, and cafes. The social state too, where everything is taken care of, everything but suicide. Yes, she is emotional. Is that a sin?

"What does a man with nothing to do do with it?" she asks.

Crusty blinks. "Come again?"

She repeats.

"Ma'am," says Crusty, "there is always nothing. Nothing is not the problem. It's when something comes along that there is trouble."

She looks again around the park. Home is only a haven from the set. The heart is a rented room. Yet half of what she and Dudley do is for charity, a kind of ersatz justice. Really, all they have is the dog. Love, otherwise, is a household appliance– better than falling into a new affair with every new leading man. Life, except for the dog, is always a new movie. Why couldn't she live in the park too? Why not, instead of being a high-priced mistress, be a bag lady?

"I tell you what, says the actress. "I'm taking you home with me. My husband will love you."

"Oh, no, Ma'am. You wouldn't do that!"

"Why not?"

"Because this is my home. I'm homeless. I live here. I'm not a dog. I'm just a bum."

"You have a soul, like I do."

"Yes, Ma'am. But I'm not housebroken like you."

The actress blushes. Again she looks at the park. The abortion in Stockholm, in the early days, is the scar of her life. She is the victim of childlessness. The victim of her own doing. The victim of voiding her womb. She did it because she could see no sense in suffering, in bringing a baby into this future of ours, a bum like Crusty. At least that was the ideology of it. Who knows. Had she merely feared for her own looks? Or her career? Or would her son have been homeless like this man?

"I'll get you a part in the movies," she says impulsively.

"Aw, shucks," says Crusty. "I ain't that good looking, Ma'am."

"You could act…!"

"Me? Act? I can't even work."

"You could be yourself."

"I am myself. But it ain't a movie," says Crusty, "Whoever I am."

She thinks hard. "Drugs. You want drugs?"

"Nope."

"You are a riddle," she says."

"Am I?"

138

Just then two young police officers strolling the Commons walk up, new on the beat. They don't know Crusty. While the actress is talking they approach slowly and ask, "Is this man bothering you, Ma'am?"

"Heavens no, Officer... I was just saying..."

"Because if he is..." they swing their sticks, jangle the iron cuff links.

"Yeah," says the other officer, "because if he is....."

"Really, Officer..." Gypsy cowers under the actress' knees and begins to growl.

"We have places for him," says the officer, then, looking at Crusty, "Don't we, Bub?"

"Maybe you'd like to lodge a complaint, Ma'am..."

Gypsy wants to bark. He wants to bite the policemen. She rises. "Maybe you would just escort me to the gate," she says to the officers.

"He won't bother you," the men say.

"It's not him," she says, "he was protecting me. It's that other gang...."

They look dubious, then accompany her toward Commonwealth Avenue.

"You better look to it, Bub," they say.

Gypsy wags his tail, And Crusty, when they aren't looking gives them a ragtear smile and doffs his invisible hat.

On Soul Street, it is always time to be moving along.

Banana specials, known as vegetarian hot dogs, are one of Crusty's street staples, a recipe taught to him by Madeleine, the bag lady. He buys a green banana at the fruit department in the supermarket and takes it to the hot dog warmer, the microwave glass case with frankfurters in the rollers and the infrared lamp.

He grabs a warm hot dog roll, spreads it with free ketchup, mustard, mayonnaise and relish, then lays in the banana. All the condiments and the roll are free. All he pays for is the banana. Sometimes he even gets to heat the banana special in the microwave.

He can also feed off free samples in the supermarket. These are usually pepperoni, cheese, cranberry juice and some kind of package desert– a jello or a pudding. Of course, the sample portions are small. Mini-portions.

In harder times, of course, he has even eaten food for cats, or dog rations. The biscuits have a lot of fiber.

Madeleine tells him to eat fiber, and when he has the spare change he buys a box of raisin bran– he likes the raisins– and a pint of milk eating the bran dry and drinking out of the carton, or sometimes pouring the milk direct into the wax paper package.

Another stop is the deli à la carte counter in the supermarket, which has a shelf life of only three days, all perishables, and he asks if they are throwing any dishes out. This way he often gets enough for Madeleine and himself, packed and wrapped, ready-to-go.

Mike's Pub is another stop, although he has to be careful here because it is for upscale clientele. But for the price of a drink, he gets to make up a snack sandwich, sometimes a hot hors d'oeuvre, from the sideboard– or a cheese potato. He doesn't take a table but stands at the bar and is out of there as soon as he has eaten. He always pays for the beer first, though.

When he can, he goes to political rallies and fund-raisers. The councilors and city candidates always have eats on hand, donated by some ethnic restaurant, and sometimes he can get a pretty good feed. All he has to do is sign in at the entryway and pretend he is a voter.

Church and neighborhood suppers are not bad either, but he needs a little cash for these. The advantage is he can usually eat as much as he wants and store up on fluids.

Another stop on Crusty's food chain is a string of downtown restaurants, where sometimes they will doggy bag leftovers for him, or he can even find a meal in the ashcan. In season, streetside pizza joints are okay too, where he can find throwaway crusts in the bin.

These institutions teach Crusty to honor the imperative of survival, an imperative that echoes on all the streets of existence. He should tell it to the Swedish actress. It signifies not only the necessity of triumphing over adversity but also living up to the self-imposed standard of survival established by generations of beggars, hoboes, tramps, and bums in America.

There is a duty to survive. Rising, Crusty feels it. The day is an improvisation on food. The banana hot dog is only one of these, called the bum's wiener. The tramp's frankfurter. It is a new kind of street cuisine.

Crusty carries a can opener with him in his jacket, too. He can eat lunch anywhere out of a can of chili. Hormel's cans are already rip tops. And microwaves are available in the convenience stores. TV dinners are precooked as if for bums and all it takes at the corner store if he minds his p's and q's is a warming up and a casual free perusal of the newspapers.

142

It is not food but uplift that comes dearest. The populace at large lives off its appetites but also its desires– shopping, besides TV, is everyman's poetry. A home has little built in comforts besides, a chair, a window, nooks and crannies that house desires and memories and habits. The bum has to do without these, and Crusty finds his living room is the city at large, and he has to know where to go if it rains. How to get a little uplift from nothing at all is a trade secret.

This is his narrative. The stoops he knows, the shelters, the back alleys, the restaurant doors, the dumpsters. Everyday he makes about 50¢ on cans, just the squashed ones he bumps into on the street. The pursuit of happiness is a dull search for survival, a corroboration of existence, and the Bill of a Bum's Rights is the right not to feel guilty when he says no.

No telephone bills. No cable TV charge. No license. No social security card. No income tax. No insurance premium. No registration. No car. No keys. Crusty finds the affirmation of life elsewhere– on a park bench, in a pigeon.

On rainy days, or in the cold, because Crusty has no home, he sometimes spends the time in St. John the Divine's, reading old magazines inconspicuously fished from the trash.

Here is a giant living room if there ever was one. It is dry. The vaults spire to whatever is above him, which is a lot, and the light is dim. He even reads the Guide to the Eucharist, and the Parish News– yes, he can read, just. No glasses even. But here, under the eye of God, he feels like a magazine himself. God fished him from the trash too, like an old newspaper. God reads him like a prayer book.

A prayer has no plot. Out on the street, there is cause and effect; the street has the logic of freedom. You get what you give, or not. Crusty, in his dim way, realizes that he is a character caught in a liturgy that either turns out good, and he gets his soup, or bad. No bed even. Not even a mat.

But here in a church, it is different. Some other plot is operative. In church, Crusty is warm not because he chose it, but because God chose. The giant vaults are arches of time. The stones are eternity. He is here in church, maybe, because he has been chosen. The moment, unlike time in the shelter, is by divine act. God made up this story, not Crusty.

He looks around the empty pews, the aisles of holiness, fearing the priest, but the house of God, even if the pews look a little like an index card filing system, is a living room. The only one outside the Public Library he has. Like the statuary, he is not entirely out of place here. The vestibule of the Lord. Strangely, he never feels himself here as a sinner.

God's stumblebum. A walking beggar. A 20th century misfit. Someone the Empire Express forgot to take along, a derelict left out of Star Wars, a bum not in the computations of cyberspace. He sits in the Church listening. Perhaps some music will swell up in the rafters and save him. Blues on the accordion. Perhaps some parish pigeons live in here. All this edifice! For what? To house the Lord; God is not homeless.

It does not, however, occur to Crusty to say a prayer. He knows no formula. What should he ask for? What are his credentials? A cipher. He is a cipher of God, past obscured, present muddled, future unsecured.

Crusty would, if the truth be known, be homeless in heaven itself, voyeur of the angels, bum in paradise looking on at all the glory, making way for the Holy Men– getting out of way, as usual, like his brother pigeon. A poor man's dove.

A few muffled old ladies are in the sanctuary with him, busy at their prayers. He has his soup with him and a coffee, the tops still on, the cups still warm. There is even a little prayer rack to sit them on, beside the hymn book. *Glory to God in the highest, and peace to His people on earth.*

Crusty has difficulty grasping the words. He reads a slow response: *A clean heart create for me, O God, and a steadfast spirit renew within me. Cast me not out of your presence, and your spirit take not from me.* Certainly the text is a little different than the regulations at the shelter. Maybe he should have been a priest. A shepherd. Lived in God's house.

At least the roof doesn't leak. No beds, however. Yes, there is no rest in the house of the Lord. But God is public; it is a public house. Why this should be so eludes Crusty. Pillars of society. Alms.

144

Society's conventions seem quaint to a person whose daily bread is on the line. Whose prayer is survival.

The hush of prayer is almost like the hush of poverty. Poverty is a funeral pall making its way down the aisle, coming to the altar, draped in black. Crusty imagines himself dead one day– no service, no coffin even. Where do the dead like him go?   Where will the ashes blow?

The door from the rectory opens. The minister, in sedate black with collar, appears, walks past the altar, down the steps, kneels, continues. Has he seen Crusty from the steeple?

He ambles slowly around passing the muffled ladies, seems headed somewhere, turns, spies Crusty, pauses, heads his way. Crusty hastily puts the cover on the coffee, crumples the bag, sits tight.

"Well, Crusty my man. Chilly outside, is it?"

Crusty nods. He should be praying. His hands should be folded. He should be on his knees.

"Tell me," says the minister. "What is your religion?"

Crusty coughs. "I have none, Sir."

"You don't believe in the Lord?"

"It's not that, Sir. It's that the Lord don't believe in me."

"So," the Reverend smiles, "But I have seen you in here before?"

Crusty nods. The Reverend eyes him with a cocked head. Something seems to occur to him, something Biblical. He is about to say, but thinks better of it. He is about to pass, caught between charity and order, between the gospel and the budget and the building fund, between the devil and the deep blue sea, but pauses at the last minute and says, "There's no eating in the Church, please."

He continues past towards the door, and Crusty gazes at the altar. Why does the man lie? Crusty has seen them all at the rail doling out the bread, their mouths wide open.

Only, Crusty wonders, why is the loaf so small?

Crusty, the world to the contrary, is going to the Ritz. Five hundred green dollars is a lot of moolah, but– in one hundred dollar bills– the Swedish actress slipped it gently to him in the park, saying, "Psychiatrists and lawyers get much more."

He sits bemused there for a whole divine hour afterward wondering what in creation to do with the money, when Madeleine, his bag lady, comes by with her three-wheeled cart and he says brightly, "We're going to the Ritz."

She looks dumbly at the money, then wistfully says, "I could buy my wedding gown."

"Let's have the honeymoon and to hell with the wedding," says Crusty, as they perk themselves up and head intrepidly across the fashionable street to the giant granite stonework hotel on the glitzy corner, with its cornices and lapidary work, somber and majestic, guarding the ancient Brahmin and vanishing fashion of balls, teas, dances, and chandeliers.

The big green and blue canopy with Ritz Carlton in gold leaf juts out over the fancy street as the polished yellow cabs glide in and out under the marquee and in front three doormen, in gray livery with green lapels, taut and tall, stand in waiting.

"Sir?" says the doorman, as Crusty and his bag lady, wheeling her dilapidated cart, prepare to enter.

Crusty flashes the bright green five hundred. "It's our honeymoon," he explains demurely.

The matronly ladies ushering in and out are fine in furs, but Madeleine, in her heavy bathrobe and rabbit trimmed boots, pulls herself up and juts her pugnacious nose in the air. A snazzy madam coming in, newly coiffured, cannot believe what she sees, but Crusty barges forward to the revolving door ushering ruddy Madeleine as he goes.

The limping cart won't go through the swinging door, and Madeleine says to the doorman, "My good man, will you see to this...?" Her whole tottering household, plastic bags, and boxes all together in a rat's nest load.

The deep oriental carpeting and glitzy show case windows greet them inside the lobby and Crusty looks at the gentlemen's clothiers window, as if he would buy a new bow tie. To the startled deskman, weary and disdainful, he huskily says, "For Madam, the best...," and waves his five hundred.

"Will you be staying...long?" asks the deskman drily.

"The royal suite. The future will take care of itself," Crusty says, as if tomorrow could change.

"Any bags?" asks the deskman airily.

Crusty, in his lumpy windbreaker, double jeans and scuffed work boots, thick stubble on his face, crusted over by weather and wear, hair soiled and tousled, points to the rickety cart that the doorman has, with difficulty, rolled in. "Just the one," he says.

"Room 519," says the deskman, wrinkling his nose. "One night."

"And Sir," he adds, giving back Crusty a few small bills and change, "if there's any trouble, we just call the police."

Crusty wishes Dr. Freed, the goateed psychiatrist at Harvard who tested him, could see him now in his grandeur, the squat porter wheeling Madeleine's grocery cart, the padded clientele gaping at the street pair as they trail in their trudging street glory to the upper reaches of the glitz, under chandeliers, past mirrors reflecting their picaresque togs and rags, past the lighting sconces and the rich tapestried walls.

148

Effortlessly the elevator whizzes the skid-row pair to their palatial room and Crusty grandly tips the porter five dollars at the thick, heavy door, picks up tubby Madeleine, and clumsily carries her across the panelled threshold of luxury into the suite with Louis the XVth chairs and armoire, a television cabinet, coffee table with Forbes magazine, and the grand double bed with pillow, quilt, and coverlet.

The door behind them rings, and the liveried valet brings in a silver bowl of fresh fruit with a card of greetings and welcome from Monsieur Xavier de Rynne, the managing hotelier, and greetings for a happy stay at the Ritz, with an invitation to have supper in the Grenadier's Room– at $80 a piece.

All Crusty has left is a 50 from the fortuitous five hundred and he rues the Cutlets of Larba la Grenadier, the Cream of Veal, and the Poulet à la Madeleine.

"What's a poulet à la madeleine?" the bag lady asks.

"That's you," says Crusty.

"Huh?"

"A pullet, a chicken, Madeleine style."

"I get it," she says. "I'm for supper. I want the oysters Rockefeller."

Madeleine already, hungry herself, looks at the menu too and then, stealthily, going to her cart and pulling out an old shoe, produces $120 and invites Crusty to supper to have the Poulet à la Madeleine.

"This is your true home," pipes Madeleine, looking cozily around. "The Ritz is really your house. You just don't know it. All these nights and days on benches, in the shelter, you earned this. Crusty, you're a gentleman. None of those homes in the suburbs are good enough for you, because the Ritz is where you really belong. That's what the world don't understand. All this luxury is nothing compared to your inner light and the suffering of the gutter."

Crusty, at this fine speech, looks embarrassed, barely comprehending Madeleine's heartfelt words, as she rifles through the ice box stashed with Belgian chocolates, mixed nuts, Champagne and cold vodka.

"The best is yet to be," says Crusty, his eyes going soft at the sight of the vodka.

He proudly takes out a vodka, pours a snifter with ice, and sits down at the mahogany desk to write a letter on the Ritz linen stationary, crowned in gold relief, to the President– the nearest relation he can think of, while Madeleine ambles into the bedroom to try on the complimentary white terry cloth bathrobe with matching slippers stamped, in gold, with the crown of the Ritz.

> *Dear Prez: writes Crusty, We are doing just dandy at the Ritz. The best is yet to come. Yours truly,*
> *Crusty*
> *P.S. Madeleine sends her greetings to the First Lady.*

Madeleine, mincing, emerges modeling the terry cloth bathrobe, doing her scant balding hair and following herself in the dazzling mirrors as she goes over and turns on the stereophonic radio to the accordion in blues, Crusty's theme song.

"Kiss me tender, kiss me sweet," the bag lady croons, "Kiss me and the heavens will be yours," and she starts eating the peanuts and cashews and peeling herself a shiny apple.

"Maybe we could still have children," she says, "How old does it stop, Crusty?" And he reads her his letter to the President. "I didn't say nuthin about the bad times," Crusty tells her confidentially, and heads in to take a bath.

"You was polite," she cries.

The china white bathroom is done in deep gold brass and Crusty, as he peels his togs, is ludicrous in the many fractured reflections and the glittering light. Even the fixtures are gold.

"This must be Jesus Christ's bathroom," Crusty calls out to Madeleine as the steam begins to smear the mirrors. She peeps in and bustingly begins to peel too, and they pour all the free shampoos, conditioners, bubble baths and after shave lotions there are on the sink and in the bath and in the cupboard into the steaming water until a great wall of white lather comes rising fluffily out of the bath, floods them, and fills up the bathroom.

"It smells like the movies," Madeleine squeals in the buff, foam up to her waist, and forgotten are all the back doors, the alleys, the stoops, the empty lots, the stench and filth, the trash bins, the dumpsters, and the smell of forlorn shelters and their daily moldering clothes.

But, for dinner, they have nothing to wear. "We'll eat in the room, on room service," says Crusty, "Poulet à la Madeleine." And he calls loftily for the meal on the bathroom phone, white and gold in its cradle.

"Do you wanna send a fax?" asks Madeleine.

"Yup." So Crusty faxes the President.

A dream is what the heart is made of. Time seems to have hidden in the closet, and the present, always the present, engulfs Crusty like a luxuriant bath. This is what he went to Greece for; this is why he went to Russia. Not for a moment does the fact that tomorrow it will be gone, like bubbles of the bath, bother him.

Tomorrow is always worse than today, and so on, to infinity, so truly, Crusty thinks, one never gets to the end of sorrow. The grave will never be as sad itself as the faces around it, and the dreaded end will never be as gloomy as dread itself.

The door rings, Crusty, in the buff, opens, and voilà– supper on wheels, in a copper warmer, just as it was when America began, before all the fast food took over, and the pop-eyed waiter, both Crusty and Madeleine naked, wheels in the Poulet à la Madeleine with its orange sauce, sets the serving things, and beats a hasty retreat to the kitchen.

This is their Last Supper– a first, of a sort. Somehow, however, it lacks the glory of MacDonald's.

Nevertheless, they eat sumptuously in their terry cloth gowns and Ritz slippers, white as Romans in togas, and on the musette play the accordion blues that seem to be Crusty's song.

"If Meathead could see me now," says Crusty.

"Or your Pop and Mom," says Madeleine.

"Or Sasha. Or Jennifer.... poor Jennifer."

151

Jennifer, it was her, at that dock in Piraeus; it flashes back on Crusty's erratic mind, and then, glowing like an angel, an image of his mother, God knows where– he can't remember, hasn't seen her in all those years, but knows it is her, and Crusty sits for a moment mesmerized as his father appears and stands next to his mother, a bum's album, in the distant past, and pretty Jennifer, and then sultry Sasha– all as if it had never belonged to him, and Crusty, picking up Forbes magazine, wonders who he is for the first time in his life, as if the magazine, with its profiles of executives, would tell him.

His name, his past, his future, are all momentarily a gigantic riddle glimmering through the glow of the foam bath and he turns to Madeleine as if he had never seen her before and wonders, as if he were in a garden, who this woman is.

"Crusty?" she says.

It is as close to love as they will ever get. There will be no magic words, no confession. The opening in his memory shuts as mysteriously as it opened and he is himself once more, a bum with Alzheimer's in the Ritz, and he looks at her not remembering his own name any more or where and what he comes from, as if a dam has burst and flooded the earth before it and left the uprooted trees, and he is back at supper, eating Poulet à la Madeleine, with the staunch, sweet bag lady that is his by the grace of some happening which Crusty only dimly knows, only dimly guesses.

A tear even comes to his eye and he bravely, galantly, flauntingly says, "The best is yet to come." Madeleine smiles bravely back.

If God were the director of the scene, he would have, at that moment, turned out the lights.

Lowry, with his bloated belly billowing between his spread legs, sits back in the dirty yellow cab and abstractedly watches the big city go by. It is amazing how the world's most powerful country, the home of the automobile, can build such ugly, uncomfortable cabs. Give him a London hack any day. He feels here that he is in the baggage compartment, enough room for a suitcase maybe.

The financial drawback is now almost complete. Lowry isn't used to losing, either. It has been slow, painful. Selling half his foreign bonds represented a concession to market psychology. The drawback is virtually inevitable, not only because the market is falling, but because he has made part of his bet in billions of borrowed funds, Still, his analytical style leads him to a costly, slow retreat– measured in days and weeks, not hours.

Yes, it is possible for him to make a bad bet. He has to admit it now. With his blue chip Wall Street reputation, he had no trouble lining up the investors to back his venture into the high-risk world of hedge funds and, he has to admit, his initial success had been dazzling. It took George Soros two decades to amass the money Lowry had put together.

It is not to say the stunning saga is at an end. But it gives Lowry a little taste of the losing hand. It reminds him of that deadbeat he took to the Union Club, used to see at the Commons, at Copley

Place— began dreaming of. A four hundred million dollar loss will set a man to rights it seems, and sometimes, as now, in the cab, he is still obsessed with the homeless man who reminds him of his grandfather.

Crusty. That was his name. Lowry remembers it now— the bum told him outside the Union Club. "No thanks," he had said when Lowry offered him a ride. "I'm already home."

To Lowry, his grandfather's is the real home. The Brahmin stronghold. He has lived in condominiums since, mostly, only now back on Beacon Hill. But not in his grandfather's house. It wasn't for sale.

As he looks back on it now, he might as well have been homeless all those years. That's how much it means to him. The heritage is going to hell, that is it. With all his money he can no longer even buy a real home: his own grandfather's. The wives, the servants, the retainers, the parlour, the horses— it no longer exists. The way of life has vanished. Value has disappeared. Quality is gone.

He asks his son, the X-generation: "Are you going into the streets?"

"Maybe," the boy says.

It infuriates him.

"Why don't you stop taking all those drugs and running around on the motorcycle and get a job."

"I don't like to work."

"You're like Crusty."

"Who's Crusty?"

Lowry mumbles. "Your great grandfather would know."

The boy dawdles. The X-generation is another unknown. Another cipher. Lowry sees this boy and Crusty in cahoots against him, somehow together dismantling the bridges, roads, and skyscrapers of America, sabotaging the financial system. Why can't the boy at least collect stamps?

Looking at his son, Lowry realizes he would like to kill Crusty. End his misery. End all misery. Philanthropist of the human soul. Misery makes a mockery of wealth, and the figures at the end of the day have no joy in them because his son looks like his great-

154

grandfather, without any of the stuffing, and his great-grandfather looks like Crusty.

Sometimes in the office, hunched over the computer monitor, Lowry himself feels like Crusty, feels he looks like him too, is incorporated by him– and he has to get up and go to the mirror to convince himself that he is Lowry. The wizard.

His son even comes to him and says, "Pop, I'm thinking of moving into the shelter."

"Why?" asks Lowry.

"It's the culture," his son says. "Being in the shelter is cool. You wouldn't have to pay me my allowance anymore. I'd have my friends and motorcycle, and we'd just, well, just live in the city. Where the action is. All the real people these days are in the shelter. Great granddad would be in the shelter himself if he were alive today."

The boy pouts a little, "Besides, drugs are no problem there. Everybody does them. You're Victorian, Pop. The world has moved on. We don't go to tea dances anymore. World War II is over. This is the millennium. What people do is take drugs and watch TV. We live in cyberspace now, and if you live in cyberspace you might as well be in the shelter, right?"

Lowry sweats it out. Then says, "Did you ever see a guy down in the Commons with stubble, a gray parka, double jeans, and scruffy work boots, looks like your great-grandfather, has a kind of wink in one eye, short hair that doesn't grow, grimy, soiled. Did you?"

"Sure Pop. I see him all the time."

Lowry knows it.

"Did you talk to him?"

"I talk to all kinds of people. What do you think I do? Life is a talk show, Pop. This isn't the 1890's."

"I don't know what you do. What did he say?"

The kid looks at Lowry quizzically. He sees he's serious, "Nothing," he says. "He said nothing. Told me he knew where the shelter was. That was all."

"Did you offer him money?"

The X-generation laughs. "You're crazy Pop. There's dozens of them. They all look like great-granddad. Why should I give him money? The state looks after him. He lives off the city. The handouts. The trouble with you is you're out of touch. You're afraid you're going to lose it all. You're afraid you'll have to talk to someone real for the first time in your life. You ought to take a vacation and go the Bahamas. Live on the beach for a while."

Lowry, in the cab, knows Crusty is in cahoots with his son in someway; his son respects Crusty, looks up to him more than Lowry. That's it. Crusty is a sort of spiritual avatar to the boy, like that Maharaji Whodunit, the Hindu flaky with the long beard in all the advertisements that the boy went to see. George Washington would turn in his grave. Lowry is possessed. He keeps thinking of ways to murder Crusty– attack dogs, strangle him on a bench, poison him, stab him, throw him out of the window of his International Tower and watch him fall to his death on the street, run him over in his Cadillac.....

"There's a good one," Lowry thinks.

Get out his Cadillac and hunt him down at some street corner, gun the machine, and take him out once and for all. No fault. No blame. No charges. No trial. It would be social justice. Nobody wants a bummer all the time. It would serve Crusty right for living free in the world and for looking like Lowry's grandfather.

The bum has no right to the family likeness. He has stolen something, a generation, from Lowry, as if looks were a patent. And now he is stealing his son, another generation, from him.

"Shad ve hed up Tremont Streed?" the driver says.

Lowry is annoyed. The Palestinian. What difference to Lowry does it make which way the driver goes as long as he isn't bothered, as long as they get there. Destination is all. After all, the man might drive him to the boondocks, rob him, and leave him on the street, like Crusty, without ID, credit cards, sans teeth, sans eyes, sans everything.

"Yes," he shouts through the plastic partition. "Take Tremont and turn at Park Street."

He sits back. His belly paunches out in front of him like a big money pouch.

"Vous sind Chef," That's pig Palestinian for "you're the boss."

Isef Shetnadandi is the cab driver. Lowry has checked the name and number. Call it a hobby. Call it security. Hack Number 1103

156

proceeding North on Tremont to Park Street Station. Lowry pretends he is reporting their location to the dispatcher. It is one of his day dreams.

But Lowry has other day dreams. One of them is being a cab driver himself. It is the only thing he can think of if all his money goes. This is the scenario: Lowry, in his Trade Towers office, calls the bank. He is checking his account. Not his assets, but his checking account.

"Lowry?" the clerk says.

"Number 3 0 4 7 5 6 3 2 1," Lowry barks.

"Just a minute, Sir,"

There is an ominous pause. The clerk returns. "We have no Lowry, Sir," says the clerk.

Lowry repeats his account number. "No," says the clerk, "we have no record of the account."

304756321. "You must be mistaken, Sir. Are you sure you called the right bank?"

Lowry calls all the banks in town. There is no account. There is no Lowry. He speaks to the managers. They have never heard of him. He has no card identifying the account– but of course he has, the plastic bank card. He calls again.

"The electronic data bank has no record of your card," they tell him. "Is it plastic?" they ask.

"Of course it's plastic," he yells.

"Tut. Tut," they say.

They have switched to electronic banking. He rushes out to the automatic teller. He is down to his last five dollars. The teller spits back his card and says he has the wrong Pin number. It cannot honor the transaction. Lowry thinks of his hundreds of millions on paper, in bonds, in securities. His house. He has signed his house over to his son. He doesn't even have a piggy bank at home.

In the cab, with Isef Shetnadandi driving, this recurrent scenario flashes through Lowry's mind and he checks his pocket to see if he has enough money to pay for the cab. Lowry is always short on cash. Goddamn Palestinian! Lowry would have to drive a cab himself if worse came to worse, which is why he wishes he could kill Crusty. Just to remove the threat. The specter of his great grandfather.

He looks up. They are at the corner of Tremont and Park, and Lowry shouts, "You fool, there's a man in the street!"

Shetnadandi is daydreaming. Palestine. He thinks he heard, "There's a Jew on the street."

Suddenly Shetnadandi is back in Jericho. The Israelis are strolling with their guns. There is small arms fire. The boys are throwing rocks, and Lowry again cries: "There's a man on the street."

Again Shetnadandi hears, "There's a Jew on the street."

By daydream, or by mistake, he steps on the accelerator. The cab jumps forward. Turn left on Park Street. Shetnadandi swerves, gunning the cab.

THUD!

At the impact on the cab, Lowry shudders, the body flies through the air, falls again. A second THUD. Shetnadandi brakes screeching to a halt.

No, there is no mistake in Lowry's mind. He knows that face. His own grandfather. A specter at the corner of Tremont and Park. Broad daylight. Palestinians and Jews, thinks Lowry, they're all the same. The money doesn't matter, he thinks, scrambling like a frog to get out the door. It's human life that counts. Odd, that.

He opens the cab, tugs his briefcase, with the records of millions in it, while Shetnadandi, groggy at the wheel, is still trying to recover. Lowry doesn't even bother to slam the door and as fast as his tubby legs can carry him waddles across the street and into the crowd at the Park Street Subway Station. He's gone.

Whoosh. A train comes by. He just gets on and heads someplace. Anyplace. A subway to oblivion.

THUD. He can still hear the body falling. See his grandfather in front of the cab. The body on the street. And it wasn't even his Cadillac. Just a beat up cab.

It is the anonymous hour, cocktail time, and most of the City is going home.

The culture is no longer drab gray and tan, but mottled by baseball hats and sports jackets with mascots and emblems, breakers, Adidas, Nike, and rubber boots. The American ethic, once a work ethic, is now a sports ethos: all comers dressed from nine to five for an athletic event, an arena, a basketball court, a rink.

Crusty, in his parka, is not so out of place, only less sporty— if the mean tilt of athletic hats, with the high, bully crown, can be called sporty. Neither does Crusty look like a workman, a telephone lineman, for instance; there is some discernible difference. A uniform of alienation, an apartness. Crusty is dressed for existence.

He is at Tremont and the corner of Park Street, obscure among the riffraff, the ethnic urbanites. He has forgotten something. There is some business he has to settle. He remembers getting the idea in the park, a brilliant idea, something that is going to save his life and change civilization, something he is going to do— for Madeleine. That is it! A future! A hope!

He is going to buy a lottery ticket!

The jackpot is up to 22 million. He even has the dollar in his pocket.

And he has thought of a number. It comes to him while he is sitting on the park bench, watching the pigeons, and he memorizes it even with his blurry brain.

304756321.

Where do numbers like this spring from in the mind of the downcast, the homeless? Large numbers. Mystical numbers full of hope.

All part of the jackpot, God's fortune that is going to redistribute chance and wealth and give the masses an opportunity of redemption. Crusty feels it in his bones; it is a winner. And he has never played the lottery before. Beginner's luck. He even gets anxious that he must get to the machine before the draw.

It is Friday. Traffic is heavy. The lords and residents of Big City are on their way home, to their identities, in this multimillion society of the urban dream, headed, home to supper, TV, love, and sleep.

Crusty crosses the street carefully. He has seen the death of so many pigeons in the city that he has come to believe he will himself be run over some day, knocked to oblivion by a reckless car, a random death– like the lottery. But he is determined to buy the ticket first.

He makes it across the street to the convenience store, enters, still rattling the winning number off in his mind, and approaches the counter.

"Jackpot. 22 million," barks the clerk. And Crusty steps up, putting his dollar on the counter.

The clerk stands, fingers poised over the keys, and Crusty, with that literal difficulty of his, the blurred mind, recites the numbers of Lowry's private bank account "304756321!"

The chances of Crusty hitting on Lowry's bank account number are 100 billion to one, greater even than the chances of winning the lottery itself.

What osmosis of numbers connects these two men, that Crusty plays Lowry's account number? No one shall ever know, not the Founding Fathers, not even God. It is simply the strange symbiosis of rich and poor, a statistical accident of America, that leads to one of the weirdest probability accidents of numbers in the history of the human earth.

Now the machine whirs, its little ratchets spurting forth the ticket, 304756321, with little plaintive ticks like the report of a ticker tape. And the ticket, long white printed strand of hope, pops up. Like toast. Like a jack-in the-box. Like a roulette ball.

"Could I have a pen, please?" Crusty asks.

The clerk hands him the pen, says, "Now don't go changing any of the numbers."

Crusty turns the ticket over and writes, "For Madeleine." He folds the ticket over and puts it in his inside shirt pocket, over his heart.

"What are you going to do with the money?" the clerk asks.

Another customer snarls, "Yeah, wreck your life."

But Crusty says, "Madeleine will know best. She deserves it."

"Yeah," says the clerk," Don't we all."

"Not me," says the other customer. "I don't want a headache. Look at how many winners shoot themselves."

But Crusty is unperturbed. He pictures Madeleine in paradise, in the winner's circle, a palm tree blowing in the wind, the warm air playing on the lapping waters, the moon, music, the blue lagoon– nothing more, not even a house, a home, he wouldn't know what more to picture than a grass hut.

Maybe, with inflation even, twenty million dollars could buy that. A fresh fish is frying in the coals in front of the grass hut. That's it. Ice cold vodka in a coconut. And the evening star, winking.

Being a winner is new to Crusty, and he is light hearted when he steps out of the convenience store into the street. The corner of Tremont and Park. He crosses.

Opposite him is a baby carriage on the loose rolling into the traffic in front of him. Crusty, winning ticket to the lottery in his pocket, realizes that it is up to him. The black mother on the other side of the curb hasn't even noticed that her carriage is rolling into the street. She is talking to two girl friends.

Twenty-two million dollars is a lot of money. Crusty thinks that, seeing the baby carriage– and what is a baby? He is filled with consternation– should he save the baby, or save the money?

The carriage is rolling freestyle toward him. All of a sudden someone honks. He dashes forward. Grabs the carriage. The baby begins to cry. He yanks it around and pushes it huff-puff to the curb. The black lady still hasn't noticed, but turns now.

"I declare," she says, as she sees the bum trolleying her carriage. Behind him, the traffic screeches to a halt. "Oh," cries the black lady. "The dolly. She lost her dolly."

And sure enough, a big ragamuffin doll has dropped into the street, looking for all the world like Madeleine.

"Save the dolly, oh, save the dolly," the black woman cries.

Crusty, completely unnerved, turns, sees the ragamuffin, thinks of the money again, of Madeleine, and darts galumphing back into the street. From the South a fast yellow cab is hurtling toward him.

At this moment, Lowry, totally unaware that Crusty, in his inside pocket, has a lottery ticket with his, Lowry's, bank account number on it, sees his grandfather in the street ahead of the cab, and shouts, "There's a man in the street!"

Isef Shetnadandi, the Palestinian driver, is day dreaming, and, thinking he is back in Jericho hears Lowry cry, "There's a Jew in the street."

Grabbed by reflex, he guns the cab. The yellow car springs forward, Shetnadandi swerves left toward Park Street and, just as Crusty bends over to pick up the fallen ragamuffin, whacks full into the bum.

THUD.

Shetnadandi hits the brakes, there is a screech as he comes to a stop, another thud as Crusty hits the street, and, dazed, Shetnadandi looks around in back of him to holler, "Why did you cry, 'There's a Jew in the street?' "

But the back seat is empty and the cab door is open. His bloated passenger is gone. This infuriates Shetnadandi. The whole thing is the fault of the war. The Israelis.

Everything always goes back to the Holy Land. Not in the land of Promise, not in the New World, can one escape the fate of Jericho. He looks out. The victim is motionless. Shetnadandi, however, can see that it is a bum. There is no mistaking the getup. He breathes a sigh of relief.

162

He praises Allah.

Allah be praised. At least he has not driven over a rich man. What is one bum more or one bum less? At least he didn't hit another car. Property is holy. He fishes in his pocket for his license, doesn't even bother to get out of the car. Maybe they won't even take his hack number from him.

But, because of the bum, he has lost the fare. $3.50. It will have to come out of his own pocket.

The dog pricks up its floppy ears.

The sudden alarm of a screeching ambulance siren pierces the park, its invasive decibels breaking the peace with blaring static, and Gypsy, good dog, violently jerks free the leash and scampers, before the Swedish actress can catch him, at breakneck speed across the Commons.

Gypsy cuts through the flower patches out to the Bridge of Sighs over the swan and boat pond, tearing hell bent as if the alarm were a call to all dogs, his nervous brow furrowed with some super message, leaving the bewildered actress stricken with surprise and concern. He has never done this. Not Gypsy.

Gypsy, faithful mutt, has always been a good dog, a passive dog. Now he seems to have heard the call of some canine bugle to arms. He is already out of mind and sight as she slings her bag and follows his trail.

Down by the pushcart hotdog stand Gypsy, who does not know her, alas, passes Madeleine, the bag lady, who sees the beautiful sleek mutt charging across the dangerous street, almost run over by the fast traffic heading West on Charles.

"My Lord," says bleary-eyed Madeleine to the hot dog man. She is avidly buying two frankfurters, chock filled with relish, ketchup, mustard and mayonnaise, for her and Crusty. "You'd think somebody had died."

But frantic Gypsy does not stop, even at the smell of food and rips under the old, forsaken trees to the East of the park, past the other walking dogs in the sheep field, past all the glorious smells of other beasties and old poo that would have dawdled him at any other time. Gypsy has business.

A sixth noseful sense of the divine is leading Gypsy in the anonymous hour, the hour of the siren, the hour of random death like the tolling of a bell. The golden cupola of the proud Capitol shines duskily out into this drab real estate of the public domain, a stone's throw from the legislature– Misery Corner.

It is here on a beeline Gypsy heads with a ferocious instinct driven by some call of the wild– no human thoughts in the dog's head, but prodded by the scrambled whir of the honking ambulance siren, by some kind of dog vision. Perhaps dogs and cats and horses see what humans think; it presses on them like an immediate picture, an omnipresent TV image unmediated by the abstract and second hand thought of human kind.

Past the pigeon bedrooled Civil War statuary, racing like a hungry greyhound at the track, bent on Misery Corner, his leash trailing after him, thrashing the ground; the passers by and sedate onlookers on the benches, untouched by fate, wonder if the dog has gone mad.

Fate like a prey is calling Gypsy to Misery Corner, like a high-pitched whistle that only dog ears can hear, as if Gypsy had been called from afar by his lawful master, as if it were the hour to be fed.

The beast's eyes are full of dog tears. The brown, gentle gazing eyeballs of canine loyalty are nurtured in the light like some kind of bird-wary instinct, full of a blind devotion and warm intensity that is the look that only emanates out of the animal world, like the heart captured in the body of the beast. It is all goodness, and instinct unsullied by greed, money, pride, lust, gluttony, envy and the deadly sins that rule the urban world. They are the eyes of fidelity. He does not bark.

166

But then Gypsy like a hunter arrives at Misery Corner and the doleful body, a gray blanket thrown over it, is crumpled still in the gutter, motionless, the gutter where Crusty once proudly lived– and died. It was here that he used to step down off the curb into the street and salute if a pretty girl passed by.

It was here he used to sometimes sit bedraggled, his sore feet in the drain. Now he is motionless, dumb, and mute, no more doughnut in his mouth, no more cup of coffee in his grubby hand– no more to join Madeleine in the dusky park this sad evening for the juicy hotdog she has prepared for him, and she will sit there ignorant and alone, waiting the glum passage of the lonely hours, wondering why Crusty, her bagman, has not come home.

On seeing and sniffing the slumped forsaken body, Gypsy begins to yell, and whine, races forward, tail wagging, and begins to lick Crusty's boots.

"Damn dog," a policeman swears, and gives Gypsy a kick; but whelping, he returns, cringing, fawning, and whining at Crusty's boots.

The other cop says, "Is this the dead man's dog?"

"Didn't see no dog widdim," says a passerby.

The white and red lumbering ambulance attendants pick Crusty up and roll him onto a stretcher. "Get that mutt out of the way."

Yelp. Yelp. Crusty cannot hear him now. Gypsy's is the world of life, of anxiety, of hunger, longing, yelping, but Crusty, hit by the mechanical impersonal remorselessness of the city is now an urban casualty– THUD– beyond it all and will never pat Gypsy again, never eat another hot dog from Madeleine's hand, never sleep on another mat.

Crusty, with his knapsack of soul, is already in dog heaven, which is where vagabonds go. They do not get to enter in the pearly gates of St. Peter's, but with the Fidos, the beasts of the field, the birds of the air– in that folk heaven of the group soul where Gypsy will someday join him.

They lift limp Crusty on the improved palette and roll him toward the bulky ambulance. The dusky crowd, a few stragglers, keep vigil, unaware of the American tragedy– no, stand-up comedy–

because Crusty's death is a mournful comedy. A sort of hidden laugh. His life has, after all, been a comedy of tears.

The bemused stragglers see the flashing lights, the alert of society, and eye the dead body eerily. It is always this way, the hush at the funerals and death. The becalmed public watches solemnly, morbidly, as if expecting something, a sign of an afterlife. Onlookers always think perhaps the bier will levitate, the coffin will open, a dead man will rise, Christ will walk again. It is the strangely sordid reverence of life for death. The immobility of the fallen corpse is somehow unbelievable, like war, unreal. But no corpse walks. No Christ rises. Just Crusty, limp and unbuttoned, lifted casually into the mouth of the ambulance where the quick disappear.

And the dog, the hound, yelping. As if for a lost God.

As they slam shut the metal doors, Gypsy tries to jump up and through to join the dead man on his last journey. Crusty, the vagabond, hasn't been inside a car for years. He won't even have to pay the fare. The siren whirs.

"Someone hold that damn dog." They have read the tag. The tag says Commonwealth Avenue, not Misery Corner. It is not even the dead man's dog.

"Rabies," says a passerby. There is always fear. Hatred. Distrust. Suspicion.

They hold Gypsy back. The grim reaper ambulance departs. But Gypsy chomps, breaks loose and, leash trailing, just as the Swedish actress in her fur coat arrives for an entrance at the scene of the accident, this crime against vagrancy, the dog, oblivious of his mistress, all his scent on Crusty, dashes madly down Tremont Street behind the ambulance, like a firehouse dog behind his truck, yelping and barking in the early night.

It is a long laconic ride to the deadbeat morgue down by the river, the last place of rest– a final home, ironically, for Crusty. The city supplies him at last with a bed: a cold slab for his haphazard soul.

The crazed dog runs behind the boxy ambulance, all the pitiful way, unmindful now of its dinner, of the actress, of the park–

somehow faithful to the dead beggar by some ununderstandable act of Providence. Only the speechless dog knows who Crusty is, his last link with life, his identifier, but the dog cannot say. All Gypsy can do is bark some unutterable anguish at the passing of his lonesome friend.

Crusty, in his shirt pocket, no longer even has his old tattered passport, the one of him thirty years ago. His last souvenir of officialdom. No, when Isef Shetnadandi slammed into him, and the cab hurtled him into oblivion, the bum's afterlife, the passport flipped out of Crusty's parka onto the road and was bureaucratically stamped by the passing wheels of a car.

Now it lies smeared in the gutter at Misery Corner, courtesy of the United States Department of State, forgotten, invalid, and unused, with the old 2" by 2" picture and visas, and an expiration date from long ago. Tomorrow Crusty will not travel. All he has left to identify the afterlife is a lottery ticket.

Otherwise only Gypsy still knows where and who Crusty is, and the drooped-tail and exhausted, the loyal dog is still there when they unload Crusty to his final resting place, not Arlington, not Mt. Auburn, but the City Morgue down by the old smoke stacks of the river and a night breeze rustles up and blows goodbye to the unidentified bum.

They mechanically wheel him into the house of anonymous death, of city oblivion, and outside at the gate, Gypsy, man's last friend, whimpers.

"Another bum," says the attendant, and they dump him, nameless, on the cold slab.

"Dead alright," says the other.

"Some dog out there waiting for him," the attendant answers. "Ought to shoot it and put it out of its misery."

"Yup. A dog is a loner," says the other. "Death is this man's best friend. A dog and death."

"A dog's death."

"Yup."

They place a tag around Crusty's wrist. "Nameless." And the date. So now Crusty has lost even the name; life is undressing him for a last naked departure.

"Even has a lottery ticket," says the attendant. He muses. "That would be a laugh. Dead man wins lottery. Well, it won't do him much good in the oven."

He turns the ticket over. "FOR MADELEINE."

"Yeah," says the attendant, thinking the dog is named Madeleine. "Twenty-two million for a dog." He chuckles, tears up the ticket, and drops the pieces into the yawning wastebasket.

"Well, Mr. Nameless won't be needing Lady Luck no more."

"Nope."

Outside in the haunted night, Gypsy is howling– while at the State offices of the Lottery, they button up the revenues and the numbers, turn the wheel, and a statistical computer selects the day's winner. Lowry's account; Crusty's ticket. A blind number with its eyes closed, naked in a cold locker.

304756321.

Twenty-two million American dollars for a dead number; a ticket for Madeleine, at chances of 100 billion to one. Yes, he was a gambling man.

That, for tonight, is Crusty's number. Probability has sung its song. A telephone call from fickle fate, area code Misery Corner– just a bit late.

An instant's hero, eternity's fool. For a black child, for a ragamuffin, he died.

Literary theorists and pundits say Crusty's tale cannot be tragedy, because the man was worth nothing in the first place. Madeleine, in bereavement, never knows for sure, but disagrees. No one ever told her. One day here; one day gone. She knew.

The same pundits say Crusty should have been more comic, that he did not make us laugh enough. He did not stand up flagrantly to the governor or the mayor and shout something outrageous, like, "Your honor, when did you fornicate last?" He did not do that. He did not shame us. He did not split our sides. His tragedy was not funny enough; his comedy was not sad enough.

Actually, in the last hurrah for Crusty, nobody says anything. But that is not quotable.

He dwells for three more cold days in the Morgue's compartment number 29, like an index card. His corpse a cipher as much as his life was. He is never even pulled out for viewing. No one comes to identify him under the sheet.

Outside, Gypsy the dog waits and waits. A dog's wait is a lone wait. He yelps, he whines, he crouches and slinks away at the men. He refuses to be fed.

For three days and three nights Gypsy loyally waits. A dog has no thoughts. Only his sniff. He has an instinct, an animal logic.

"Whadda we do about the damn dog?" they ask.

"Yeah. Have him taken away."

So on the third day, the day of Crusty's cremation, they call the pound. A professional dogcatcher comes with a truck, a truck a little like the ambulance that ran Crusty to the morgue.

"Whadda ya hanging round here for?" they say.

Gypsy looks at them with mournful eyes. But it is too late. They drive him off to the pound just at the same moment that in the morgue they slip Crusty's body into the oven. They put Gypsy into a kennel and give him a bowl of water and some dog food, but Gypsy is too weak to eat. Gypsy dies a day after Crusty is cremated. Then they burn Gypsy too.

But beforehand they read the tag and call the Swedish actress on Commonwealth Avenue No. 2.

"Your dog is dead," they say. "We picked him up hanging around the city morgue."

So the actress knows. If Gypsy is dead, Crusty is dead. Call it a woman's intuition. She takes her shawl and goes out in the Spring air to sit on the bench where Crusty and she had talked. She sits there puzzled by the season. All she can remember of the little he ever said was, "Ya know, I'm in love."

He doesn't tell her with whom. But he says, "Ya know, you have to have a soul to love."

Remembering that, the Swedish actress mourns her dog. At least, she thought it was the dog. A bag lady in a bathrobe with a three-wheeled grocery cart comes slowly pushing by, and the Swedish actress looks up. But she doesn't know her. They lived in the same garden, but never met.

"Why didn't he love somebody like her, and not me," the actress thinks.

But it isn't the Swedish actress that Crusty loved. Alas, it isn't Madeleine either. Yet Crusty never told her. He never said to the bag lady, "There is another woman. A girl."

172

On the third day, the flames receive his remains. There is no whimper, no yelp, no Lazarus in the fire. He comes out ashes, and the attendant rakes him up, shovels him into an urn.

But in the slippery corridor outside the mouth of the oven, the attendant slips, the urn falls, breaks, and Crusty's ashes spill on the floor.

The attendant sweeps him into a dustpan. He is going to fetch another urn, but then he thinks, "Why waste another urn. After all, the goner was a bum. Nobody is going to come for this in a million years. Why should I?"

He grins. After a while the morgue gets on your nerves. The city is full of bums. One more, one less, isn't going to hurt the economy, so the attendant, sheepishly, goes to shut the rear door, exits, and dumps the dustpan into the dumpster. Ashes to ashes, dumpster to dumpster.

"Amen," he says.

It is in this way that Crusty's remains are trucked the next morning to the Deer Island landfill in the harbor, where he is finally buried with the rest of Boston's unrecycled waste, to rot or live forever, just like an old plastic bottle, taking up a part of the sea, visited by gulls, a cemetery of political refuse, a remainder man of reject, a few gray ashes in the rest of the garbage.

Not even the worm lives here. Nothing will grow in the waste of Crusty and his surroundings; no inscription to the bum's life, just part of the six billion dollars harbor project.

Overhead the jets Crusty never flew in bring passengers in and out of the land of opportunity but his soul has no stone to mark his contribution to the 20th century.

A part of the city, as if he had been crushed rock, part of a street for removal, and nobody laid flowers on his grave, nobody remembers him, and not even he himself can. His one achievement is that in the end, now that he is dead, he believes in himself— in what he was.

And that he had a secret love. Oksana Baiul, the ice skater, is the only thing he ever truly cared for, truly aspired to, and somewhere, somehow, she is skating in a white tutu oblivious of Crusty, oblivious that he ever loved her, oblivious that she kept a homeless man's heart alive by smiling into the wind as she did her axels and lutzs and held her pretty fingers out like a bird.

Crusty can remember no more. He is too ashy and groggy in the ground to remember even Madeleine. Unless memory, like a photograph, is freed by cremation and lives on in afterlife like a butterfly rising into the ozone and disintegrating into the sun.

Crusty is now part of the harbor. Part of the urban waste disposal. Part of the land reclamation. The world's gold is 99% dust, sometimes an ounce of it in a ton, but how much did Crusty's ashes weigh in the refill?

Who would, beside Madeleine, ever sift for this soul that was part of America on the verge of a new millennium. Beggars don't freeze their bodies. Bums don't look forward to resurrection. There is no legacy, no estate, no heir. No obituary. The meek give themselves to the earth without qualifications, without reservations, without conditions.

No lawyer writes the last Will and Testament of Crusty, yet something endures. The love for Oksana. Madeleine's love for him. But more than this.

Some child has seen this face and remembers. It was Crusty who used to hang out at the corner. He is the figure of a visual question mark of the whole civilization, a reminder of the vanity of riches but also the vanity of social welfare and Medicaid, a counter image of the American dream.

He is the tramp without the top hat, without the cane, without the enormous floppy shoes, without a stick over his shoulder carrying his belongings in a satchel, without the credit on the marquee, without a smile.

Charley Chaplin's smile outshone the Great Depression, but Crusty's face is a mouth with the smile worn off it. The mouth that never kissed Oksana. One thing remains: obduracy.

It is stronger than survival. The face, too, is in some way human, like an old Rembrandt, commenting beyond words on fate.

Some child, oh, yes, some child has seen that face. Some child remembers. Some child will know more about life than he or she will ever learn at school, at the bank, at the movies, because he or she has seen Crusty once at Misery Corner.

The expression, despite the cars, the causeways, the highways, the skyscrapers, hangs on. It will haunt the child for a lifetime, the way Lowry was haunted by his grandfather, and be a ghost in the system of capitalism and the free market as long as there are streets and corners and Crusties.

Christ's countenance, they say, was preserved on the cloth of Veronica when he stooped on his way up the Via Dolorosa bearing the crucifix to his own death. Crusty's face, too, is preserved in the minds of millions of passersby.

There is no need to sentimentalize; no need to say he was more than he was, different than he was— he was never on TV, never in People Magazine, never in the movies, not even in his own family album. Now he is part of the landfill. God bless!

He had his price, It was 25¢.

He haunted the city. He stood there as if we had all lost the belief in Santa Claus, abandoned by his reindeer, his sleigh stolen, his robes turned to rags, his white beard besmirched, ragged, grimy, and stubbly. His hand is out still, not in a gesture of friendship, not ready to shake, but posing there like the question of who are you?

What have you got to give?

25¢. Not much.

A voice, hoarse, coarse, timid, beyond despair, beyond hope, beyond disappointment, a voice remembered by some little child of the future itself, holding Daddy and Mommy's hand and innocently pronouncing a kind of judgment on the whole soul of the street. Soul Street.

"Spare a quarter, Mister?"